Sherlock Holmes

and

The Man Who Lost Himself

By the same author

Sherlock Holmes and the Egyptian Hall Adventure
Sherlock Holmes and the Eminent Thespian
Sherlock Holmes and the Brighton Pavilion Mystery
Sherlock Holmes and the Houdini Birthright
Sherlock Holmes and the Greyfriars School Mystery

Sherlock Holmes
and
The Man Who Lost Himself

Val Andrews

**BREESE
BOOKS
LONDON**

First published in 1997 by
Breese Books Ltd
164 Kensington Park Road, London W11 2ER, England

ISBN: 0 947533 70 2

Typeset in 11½/13½pt Caslon by
Ann Buchan (Typesetters), Middlesex
Printed and bound in Great Britain by
Itchen Printers Ltd, Southampton

I t was in the autumn of 1903 that I was staying with my old friend Sherlock Holmes at our old rooms in Baker Street. At that menage (organised so smoothly and unobtrusively by the good Mrs Hudson) Holmes seemed unwilling to accept that I had ever been away. But then he had never shown much concern for my occasional absence and reappearances, my old room ever ready with fresh linen. Within half an hour I would tend to forget that I had been away from 221B Baker Street.

Soon after this latest reappearance of mine, Sherlock and I were dining upon a game pie so enterprisingly produced by the housekeeper. I complimented her upon it, saying, 'Upon my word, Mrs Hudson, you are a wonder.'

She smiled sweetly. 'It has always been a pleasure to cook for you, Doctor, for you have such a healthy appetite. Not like Mr Holmes, for there are times when he scarce eats enough to keep a sparrow alive. I'm so glad to see that you have helped him to regain his appetite.'

Holmes smiled and responded, to the extent that his reclusive nature allowed, 'The combination of this excellent game pie and the company of my good friend have combined to work wonders, Mrs Hudson.'

Doubtless the good lady had a delicious dessert up her voluminous leg-of-mutton sleeve, but alas we were not to see it, with our repast being interrupted by a most irritatingly urgent pulling upon the door bell. The good lady sighed heavily, exclaiming, 'Botheration and fiddlesticks! Pray excuse my strong words, gentlemen, but Billy has the evening off and Hudson is at his tavern. I must go and see who is making such a clatter.'

The housekeeper placed down her tray and her industrious feet were soon heard upon the stairs. The front door was opened to allow the agitated strains of a man's voice to be heard. These were followed by those of the good lady's returning footsteps. Holmes said, 'Whilst I cannot make out his words, our caller is an educated man in considerable torment for his voice is raised in a manner which does not match his refinement. He has no appointment for I am not expecting anyone, therefore his business is urgent. Listen to his tread, it is heavy and uncontrolled like that of a drunkard, though I doubt if that is what he will prove to be.'

After Mrs Hudson had gone through the niceties of announcing him, Professor Mainwaring entered the room, proving to be in a condition that can only be described as one of distress. He was a tall man though bowed over by anxiety, and his luxuriant red hair stood on end as if it had not had the attention of brush or comb for some days. His dress, though rumpled, suited his title, being sombre in the extreme. Despite the autumn bluster he boasted no hat, greatcoat, nor even a cane. Had he tried to enter an establishment where his title might normally have made him welcome it is doubtful if he would have been admitted. Holmes rose from his seat at the table and, shaking our visitor by the hand, managed almost in the same movement to steer him towards the most comfortable chair near the fireplace. The blaze threw shadows onto the professor's face, emphasising his anxiety of expression.

Holmes spoke in kindly tones as if calming a terrified horse, 'Come, sir, you are all in; pray sit and rest awhile before you attempt to speak further. I am Sherlock Holmes and this is my friend and colleague Dr Watson, before whom you may speak freely as soon as you are ready to do so.'

As a medical man I was more than a little concerned for our visitor and poured him some brandy from the decanter. He nodded thankfully, drinking a little of it, then speaking in agitated tones. 'Mr Holmes, Dr Watson, please forgive my intrusion and also my appearance, but I am not the man I was, you see. I have, to put it bluntly, quite lost myself. I have neither eaten nor slept for forty eight hours and in all of that time this is possibly the only occasion on which I have even been seated.'

Holmes glanced enquiringly at me, pointing to the remains of our meal, as if to ask for my medical opinion. I understood his enquiry perfectly and spooning some of the pie onto a clean plate served it to Mainwaring on a tray along with a cup of hot, sweet coffee. He smiled gratefully, at once starting to eat and drink. But he managed to speak to us, urgently, between mouthfuls and gulps, 'Mr Holmes, I am at my wits' end. I have been to the official police who seem quite unable to help me in my dilemma . . .'

Holmes reassured him, 'If you can tell me what this dilemma is, I promise that I will do whatever I can to help you. Tell me your story, cutting all corners, but start as near to its beginning as is possible and practical.'

What the professor then related turned out to be possibly the most amazing story that I had ever heard, even allowing for my twenty-year association with the world's only consulting detective. Mainwaring spoke urgently but coherently, 'Until last Monday, Mr Holmes, I resided quietly with my wife in a rather secluded house near a village in Surrey, not far from Reigate. My wife, Mary, on Monday evening, complained of feeling extremely unwell. She is delicate but her condition usually requires only medication of a sedative nature. However, I did feel that she seemed unwell enough to warrant a visit to the doctor. I drove her to the surgery in my dog-cart, a distance of only a mile or two. The door to Dr Royston's house was ajar, so we went straight in and to the waiting room where we found no one to be waiting. The door of the doctor's office itself was slightly ajar so we assumed that we had luckily caught the medic just in time. My wife entered the office, then glanced back at me with a reassuring smile and I assumed that all was well. She closed the door after her and I just sat and patiently waited. I say patiently, and this for the first hour was true. But when I again consulted my watch and found that I had been waiting for the better part of an hour and a half I began to feel restive. Then eventually I rang the bell which would summon the nurse who walked through the door from an ante-room and asked me what I wanted, telling me that the doctor had departed two hours earlier. I told her that this was impossible as my wife was with him at this very moment. I asked if there was another way out of the doctor's office, to be told that there was not. I rushed and pushed open the door of the consulting room to find it quite empty.'

At this point Holmes interrupted, almost apologetically.

'You are really quite sure that there was no other means of exit or entrance?'

'Why no, not as far as I could discover. There was a small barred window but no other door nor yet a large cupboard within which anyone or anything could be concealed. I was at this point quite bewildered but would soon become even further confused and angry when the nurse denied the possibility of Mary having even entered the room. She even questioned her existence!'

I felt bound to enquire, 'Surely if your wife was a regular patient her records would have been on file?'

'My own very next thought Dr Watson, and I demanded to see her file card or dossier. The nurse went through all the surgery records and seemed to prove to me that no record of a Mary Mainwaring existed. Indeed, to be truthful it appeared to me that a very few patients appeared to be on record. Mary had always previously been to the doctor's on her own, usually just to renew her prescription for sedative tablets. At this point, gentlemen, I suppose I did make some sort of a scene. I demanded to see Dr Royston but was told that he had left some hours earlier, and by now had departed to stay with some friends in London. The nurse began to accuse me of being a lunatic. Perhaps you think the same, Mr Holmes, in which case I am finished.'

Holmes shook his head, looking enquiringly at me and I did the same. As a medical man I could see that our visitor displayed none of the classic symptoms of mania or lunacy. We reassured him, plying him with more coffee and begging him to continue with his narrative. 'Well, I then did the only thing that I could think of to do, returning to my house, the Willows, hoping that I would find my wife safely back there. Perhaps I might find it all to be some ghastly dream or hallucination. I drove my poor old horse furiously so that the fairly short journey became even quicker.

Then, home having been reached, I did not even stop to secure my horse and dog-cart, fairly leaping up the gravel path to my front door. I found to my total amazement that my key would not fit the door lock. It was as if the very lock itself had been changed, which indeed is what I now believe to have been done. I walked round to the tradesmen's door at the side, only to find that the big old key would not open that either. There was one key left on my ring, that to my workshop, which is an outbuilding. When I failed to gain entrance to the workshop I gazed in through its window, seeing to my amazement that all of my equipment had been removed and replaced with garden implements and plants in earthenware pots. Then, to add to my troubles, a huge and horrific dog of the mastiff variety came upon the scene, threatening me with a terrifying snarl. A man appeared and secured the dog by its spiked collar, before it could actually attack me. He was a big and surly brute who demanded to know who I was and what my business might be. Almost apoplectic with rage by this time I informed him that he and his dog were trespassing on my property. But he said that he had leased the property for the last three years and that if I did not remove myself he would release the dog and let it deal with me. Quite unable to think what else to do I made for my dog-cart, intending to take myself to the nearest police station. But to my dismay I found that neither horse nor cart were anywhere to be seen. The uncouth man shouted after me, accusing me of being a tramp, a role for which I might well now qualify, but not at that point in time. I walked to the village and consulted the one and only policeman who took me seriously enough to drive me back to the Willows in a police vehicle. But then the whole dreadful nightmare was re-enacted with the uncouth man convincing the policeman that I was a dangerous lunatic. I was not arrested or detained, but told by the policeman to clear off and not to go near the Willows again. But it was my home, and I had nowhere to do. I had no near neighbour or relatives to turn to. I slept out in the woods, or rather tried to. The following morning I walked to Reigate where I seemed to remember were the offices of the agent who had leased us the property for the past several years. But my wife had always handled all my business affairs, including finance, for I am inclined to be somewhat vague about such things. The agent denied all knowledge of us and when I got angry he threatened to send for the police . . . of whom I had endured quite enough, had I not? So there I stood, Mr Holmes, in the clothes I was wearing, am wearing. I had lost my wife and even my own identity, my home, my work and whatever money my wife had care of. I had some small change in my pocket, enough to take the train to London. Mercifully, I remembered your name and address and reputation. You assisted an old friend of mine many years ago, who has since left the country. There is nobody else I can turn to, sir, so if you turn me away I swear I will take myself off to the Embankment and cast myself into the Thames. I cannot swim so it seems a good way out.'

Professor Mainwaring's narrative tailed off. The refreshment we had provided seemed to have given him just enough strength to tell us what he had and no more, for now he was spent. As for Holmes, I could see that he was moved as well as intrigued by this strange story that had been presented. He filled his favourite clay with the dark shag from the Turkish slipper. I had seldom seen him forgo the use of tobacco for quite so long, illustrating how rapt had been his attention. But he lit the pipe now with a vesta.

'Professor, I have seldom if ever been presented with such an enigma, certainly none with such serious consequences for the principal involved. I will help you in every way I can. There are a great many questions that I need to ask you, but refuse to put you through any further ordeal at this point in time. Come, Watson, put your spare pyjamas and razor into a carpet-bag, along with some clean linen and anything else that occurs to you. Then take the professor across the street to the private hotel where I am known and my credit good. After a good night's rest, sir, the world will seem a better place and we will discuss your future over a good breakfast which you will take with us here.'

I did as Holmes bade me, escorting Professor Mainwaring to the small hotel where the manager was used to taking in an occasional lost sheep from 221B.

On my return to the rooms I found Holmes seated upon the floor, his clay pipe having seemingly contributed more smoke than had the fire. He was in a rather trance-like state, usually indulged by him only when rather more information had been gained than that provided by our client. I said as much and he replied, 'Come, Watson, although it would have been cruel to question a man on the edge of nervous collapse, certain acts have already emerged which are worthy of considerable thought. His occupation, for example, may have much bearing on the whole matter.'

'I do not remember that he actually told us what it was. The only clue would be the presence of a workshop in the grounds of his house.'

Holmes knocked his pipe out into a small bowl that had been made for a quite different purpose and captioned 'A Present From Brighton', which may well have held sentimental value to our long-suffering landlady. He continued, 'Did you not notice the shape of his thumbs? That he is an engineer is evident from the shape of those members and certain other aspects of his hands. These things tell me that he has followed this occupation for several years at least, yet there is nothing about him to suggest that he works at a menial or low-paid occupation. Moreover, he introduced himself to us with the title of professor. What does all this suggest?'

'Oh, I don't know . . . perhaps he is a college tutor with a hobby concerning model engineering.'

'A college professor who has no one else to turn to in his hour of need save a sleuth known to him only by reputation?'

'Retired, perhaps?'

'Oh come, Watson. The man is perhaps five and thirty. Think, man, you know my methods.'

'Could he be a professor of music or philosophy?'

Holmes put me out of my misery, saying, 'No, Watson. You are delving into areas of pure guesswork. Ours is an exact science rather than a speculative occupation. Examine the facts; he is both a professor and an engineer. Add the hint of a hermit-like existence and I am led to believe that he is an inventor. It is possible that he has made some sort of discovery revolutionary enough to attract the attention of unscrupulous piratical persons. These persons may even be in the pay of some foreign government. In fact, this thought seems a quite logical one considering the drastic nature of the enterprise. I cannot imagine any native industrial company that would indulge in practices drastic enough to deprive a man of his invention, his wife, his home and his very identity! Come, my dear fellow, this promises to be one of the most interesting problems that we have ever been called upon to solve. I would be happier, however, if there were less evil in it. Oh, mark my words, Watson, evil there is here, as I feel sure we will discover.'

On the following morning I arose rather later than I had intended to discover Professor Mainwaring already seated at breakfast with Sherlock Holmes. He looked quite a different man from the wild-haired intruder of the night before. He had obviously been partaking of a hearty breakfast and he rose and shook me by the hand, saying, 'Dr Watson, I slept like a child from sheer exhaustion. Now I feel slightly less confused and so immensely relieved that Mr Holmes is taking my predicament seriously rather than considering me as some kind of maniac.'

Holmes, who had acknowledged my entrance to the room with a wave of his hand and without even bothering to turn his head in my direction, spoke to Mainwaring. 'Tell me, Professor, what is the nature of this latest invention upon which you have been working?'

Mainwaring started, and asked, 'How did you know that I was an inventor, for I have said nothing to you yet of my occupation.'

Sherlock Holmes explained a little about the conversation which he and I had held the night before and how we had built a background from the very little that we did know about him. When he had recovered from his surprise the professor explained, 'You are quite right, of course, I am an inventor, an engineer, although my degree is of one in science. For many years I have shut myself away, seeing nobody save my wife, that I might have the peace and quiet which I need to follow my bent. During the last ten or twelve years I have produced an improved typewriting machine which enables the operator to actually see what he or she is typing without recourse to raising the top, and a greatly advanced grass-cutting appliance enabling the small householder to cut his own lawn. These machines, or rather the sale of their patents, have made me financially independent. As I am a duffer at finance I have always allowed my wife to handle money matters. Everything of a financial or business aspect is in fact in her name.'

He started a little at his own words, as if they raised a fresh aspect of difficulty. He continued, 'By jove, my wife's disappearance is going to present me with yet another problem. Though perhaps the investigation of her bank account might assist with your enquiries.'

My friend looked rather grave as he said, 'Possibly, sir, but please for the moment continue to tell us of your inventions.'

'Well, my current work has been the development of an engine of the internal combustion type. It has a cooling system, quite revolutionary.'

I said, 'Surely, Rolls-Royce or Mercedes would not stoop to the theft of an invention?'

Judging from Mainwaring's expression it seemed to me that the thought of the theft of his invention had not yet crossed his trusting mind. But my remark struck a chord with Holmes, who nodded and asked, 'Can this engine be used in anything of greater importance than a private motor car?'

'Why, yes. My whole purpose in its development was directed towards aviation. You will be familiar, gentlemen, I feel sure, with the existence of flying machines, other than those that are mere gliders, I mean the power-driven variety. Well, at the present time these are only able to remain airborne for a very few minutes and will not rise to any great height. But an aeroplane (as they are sometimes called) fitted with my new engine which is lighter than those in use with a new cooling system, might manage half an hour and gain a height of several hundred feet.'

I enquired, 'Would that make your invention of international importance?'

Holmes fairly pounced upon my words. 'Really, Watson, what a question. Such a machine could cross enemy lines from above during time of war, dropping explosives and still having time to return to its base, or aerodrome as I believe these are called. Can you imagine what effect their ownership might have had on the recent South African conflict had the Boers had access to such an invention.'

I had of course heard about flying machines, but had never realised that they were to be taken seriously. Obviously Holmes had, and he continued, 'Professor, I believe then that we have at least found a possible motive for what has happened to you. Tell me, who beside yourself might have had knowledge of that which you were working upon?'

'Absolutely no one, apart from Mary, and I never talked to her much about my work, for she is such a goose concerning machinery.'

Sherlock Holmes pushed his breakfast plate away having made, for him, quite a decent job of dealing with it. Then he drained his coffee cup and consulted his hunter, saying, 'Watson, we must go next to Poolford and make a few enquiries. Professor, you may stay here and rest yourself and I will tell Mrs Hudson to take care of your meals and needs. Should we be long detained, you know your way to the hotel and we will contact you as soon as we return.'

'Thank you, Mr Holmes, but dare I ask how you knew that my home is, or was, in Poolford? For I mentioned only that I resided not far from a village near Reigate.'

My friend was slightly impatient, 'Come, sir, the chalk dust that was on your boots when you arrived last night is found mainly in that of all localities near Reigate. In fact whilst we are gone it might amuse you to read my monograph upon the subject of localised soil deposits and their study for the benefit of crime detection. You will find it on the shelf next to a red scrapbook. Meanwhile, I want you to give me the name of your wife's bankers, the address of the agent who leased her the property and of course the address of the disputed residence. Inform me too where I can find the surgery of the elusive doctor.'

Holmes wrote all of this information swiftly into his leather-covered notebook and we left the fog of Baker Street for the autumnal chill of the Surrey countryside.

The third cab on the rank rattled us off to Victoria Station from whence we took the train to Reigate. That delightful market town could have held many delights for me, as one apt to browse, but Holmes firmly directed our footsteps in the direction of Lorrimer's Bank, which was within the very shadow of the railway station. There the manager, having first informed us that all financial affairs of his customers were strictly confidential, actually denied the existence of an account under the name of Mary Mainwaring. We could not press the point, for in a bank the manager's word is law, rather like that of a chief inspector at Scotland Yard. As we were leaving, Holmes could not resist saying, 'Come, sir, do not worry. Perhaps that last depositor will return to the arrangement where he banks his money with you?'

He started, 'How did you know that I was working upon the return of a difficult customer, sir?'

Holmes laughed, 'The red ink upon your fingers, sir, indicates its own story. Your customer is in the red, as the saying goes. A man in your position would have washed away the red ink within the half-hour.'

But a stone's throw from the bank we found the offices of 'J Arthur Saunders, Sons and Co' which proved to be housed in the centre of a small parade of shops and businesses. We entered and I took my cue from the master actor, Sherlock Holmes. He spoke to the man who sat behind the main desk. 'Good morning. My name is Martin Witherspoon and this is my colleague Professor Simpson. We are scientists looking for suitable residence in the area, with outbuildings in which we can conduct our experiments. Whilst our work is neither illegal nor yet dangerous it can be bothersome to near neighbours; nasty smells and the like; so we need something just a little off the beaten track.'

I can only describe Holmes's manner during his oration as precious and I tried to imitate it in my new role as an eccentric scientist, twittering quite so and the like. The clerk was a burly young man with a somewhat distracted manner, who replied, 'Mr Witherspoon, Professor Simpson, we are not issuing new leases because we are going out of business. We are, however, disposing of the freeholds of some of our properties and I have one that might be ideal for your purpose, being roomy, secluded and with outbuildings. The present occupier who has leased it from us for a number of years is also leaving . . . that is, he has already left.'

He showed us a drawing of the residence which I noted bore a nameplate, the Willows. Holmes passed the sketch to me as he perused the prospectus. I twittered suitably, 'On the surface it appears to be just what we are looking for. We would like to view it, eh, Witherspoon?'

Holmes, growing in enthusiasm for his impersonation of an affected scientist, nodded excitedly. The clerk took up his hat and greatcoat, saying, 'Then I will take you there directly, gentlemen. It will not, I expect, make you nervous if we ride there in my motor car?'

We both twittered and shook our heads. The letting office was left in the hands of a red-haired young lady with thick-lensed spectacles.

Only twice before had I travelled in a motor car. The first of these had been referred to as a horseless carriage and had been preceded by a rider on a horse, waving a red flag. The second had been very much later but almost as alarming. But the machine owned by Mr Saunders proved to be of a rather more reliable nature. Its engine fairly purred as we sped along the Reigate road in the direction of Poolford. Once clear of Reigate itself we passed few domiciles, although one that we did seemed to catch Holmes's attention and I caught a fleeting glimpse of a doctor's plaque upon its gate.

The Willows lived up to its description, given to us by Professor Mainwaring. The furniture was still in place, as were the rugs and curtains. The agent mentioned a price of around five hundred pounds for the freehold which at that time and place was a bargain. After a perfunctory inspection of the house, Holmes asked to see the outbuildings and we were shown first what Saunders referred to as the potting shed. This proved to be a rather large sectional wooden building, full of garden implements and potted plants, which I assumed to be Mainwaring's workshop. There were oil stains upon the path outside the building which I thought to be normal where implements and machinery were involved. Next we were shown the stable and carriage house which was a rather larger and more imposing building. There were signs of the recent occupation by a horse, but no sign of any carriage nor cart. Holmes peered around as closely as he dared, especially at the partially paved frontage to the building. Where the paving existed there were oil stains of the kind that we had seen in the shed. Where it did not, there were deep ruts made by carriage wheels, the lubrication of which could have been responsible, I thought, for the oil stains.

Mr J Arthur Saunders assured us of the need for prompt action if we really wished to purchase the property, the occupying tenant having already departed. Moreover, he, J Arthur Saunders, was also about to leave the district, as already inferred. Holmes explained that he had neglected to bring his card case, having left it at his home in Cadogan Square; the mention of which fictitious address produced a gleam of greed in the agent's eyes. He told us that there might be certain extra charges which he had neglected to mention. Holmes nodded and said that his solicitor would make the arrangements. We were offered a lift back to Reigate in the car but this, to my dismay, Holmes declined, saying, 'My friend and I would like to walk those few miles, not only for the beneficial exercise involved but in order that we might familiarise ourselves with an area in which we could well soon reside.'

As soon as Saunders had wished us good afternoon and departed in his motor car I asked Holmes concerning his observations. He said, 'Watson, the carriage house has been used as a shelter for a motor car and very recently. After all, Mainwaring owned no such contraption and the oil is fresh.'

'I saw it, but took it to be a sign of carriage wheels being lubricated.'

'No, such oil is of a thinner type; moreover there are thick rubber tyre tracks among those of the cartwheels in front of the building. I also noticed traces of a similar thick oil outside Mainwaring's workshop.'

'What do you deduce from these facts?'

'I will tell you later, Watson, when we have both had a little time to consider. You know my methods and I will look forward to hearing your conclusions.'

I grunted and then asked, ruefully, 'Why have you landed us in the middle of nowhere, Holmes, with a three-mile walk back to civilisation?'

'Come, Watson, we are both stoutly shod and I need to examine the district. Most particularly I want to visit the doctor's surgery and there is no need for friend Saunders to know of this.'

'What do you make of him, Holmes?'

'Saunders? A rogue, Watson, a rogue! I read it in his face and from his actions; and in the anxiety he shows to quickly dispose of the property, yet the greed which he could not resist at the mention of my fake address in Cadogan Square.'

We strolled along the lane which led us back to the main Reigate road. It was easy enough to imagine how Professor Mainwaring could have resided at the Willows without becoming known to his tiny number of neighbours, with the entry to the lane half-concealed by thickets, brush and undergrowth. Indeed Saunders's car had been steered into the lane only with some difficulty. A brisk walk along the Reigate road brought us eventually to the other isolated house, the one with the name plate of Dr Royston. A smaller notice, handwritten upon a sheet of paper, had been partly pasted over the details of the surgery hours. It read, 'Dr Royston has removed to London'. We pulled at the door bell but gained no response. I said, 'Holmes, it occurs to me that there is significance in the coincidental closing of Saunders's office, removal of Dr Royston for London and the departure of the so-called tenant at the Willows.'

Sherlock Holmes had always been at his most irritating in sarcasm. 'Oh, Watson, you latch on to things so quickly! Of course these things are connected, but I would dearly like to see the inside of this so-called surgery. A strange locality for a general practitioner, do you not think?'

'I imagine he would be lucky to encounter a patient in a week.'

'Exactly. Remember, Mainwaring told us that there were no patients waiting for evening surgery. His wife was able to walk straight in to see Royston. But *he* did not see Royston, only a nurse and she much later.'

Holmes took from his pocket a wire loop which I

21

recognised as a homemade pick lock. With a few deft movements he demonstrated to me that, had he been inclined, the great Raffles would have needed to look to his laurels. Unlawfully entering the house made me a trifle timid, but for Holmes it was all part of the day's work. He chided me for my timidity, 'Come, Watson, don't lurk about. It is part of our trade that we need to make the occasional illicit entry.'

Most of the furnishings and fittings were still present in the rather uninteresting little house, as we discovered during our examination of each room in turn, though we were mainly interested in the ground floor which contained the rooms that Mainwaring had described. The lounge, which had served as the waiting room, still had its square of chairs, whilst the door at the far end betrayed through four screw holes that it had been the surgery. On our right as we faced that door we saw another, the one through which the nurse must have entered to inform poor Mainwaring that his wife was a figment of his imagination, or words to that effect. Investigation in the 'surgery' revealed no obvious means of escape, the only window being small and heavily barred. There was no other door or place of concealment, it was just as Mainwaring had described. We examined the chairs and the desk, pushing back its rolltop and opening its drawers. In one of these we found a small box marked 'Leichener Theatrical Powder . . . Blonde', and also a few long red hairs. These, Holmes claimed, might well have been from a wig, being not human hair but horsehair. He placed the hairs into a small envelope which he had taken from his pocket.

'Theatrical make-up materials, Watson, powder and dyed horsehair. Perhaps Dr Royston was an actor in his spare time, of which we have established he must have had a great deal.'

But it was the fact that the doctor and Mary Mainwaring had evidently both disappeared without trace from the surgery that intrigued Holmes's imaginative processes the most. The bars at the window and lack of any other sort of egress or hiding place created a puzzle indeed. In a more thorough examination we took up the rug, having first moved the desk in order to facilitate this. This action revealed an all but concealed panel which proved indeed to be a hinged trapdoor. I took out my pocketknife and with its implement intended for the removal of stones from a horse's hoof I assisted Holmes in raising it. Holmes peered down through the aperture that its raising had created, then dropping to his knees he struck a vesta in order to investigate the dark space beneath. He raised his head, saying, 'It is a cellar, Watson, and the drop is only about eight feet, yet I am determined to ensure my ability to climb out again before making the drop.'

Eventually, he espied some sort of small ladder below so decided that we should risk a descent which we did, without difficulty or real injury. (I did, however, manage to twist my ankle, but it was not a real sprain. Holmes tore only his jacket.) We looked about us by the light of a series of struck vestas, eventually discovering a candle which made things easier. There was indeed a ladder which would make our return quite simple, yet there was nothing much that attracted our attention within the cellar until we discovered a second trapdoor some twenty feet from the one through which we had entered.

Holmes spoke at last. 'No need for us to raise the second trap, Watson, because we know roughly its position. It is in the room from which the nurse emerged to inform Mainwaring that neither his wife nor yet the doctor were present. At that time I suppose that both of them could have still been in the cellar, but I wonder how they managed to close the trap and rearrange the rug so that Mainwaring would not see it?'

He took the ladder, placing it against the wall so that he could climb and manipulate the trap, pulling the rug around until he was sure that it could be manipulated to drop with the flap. Then we emerged by way of the ladder back into the room that had been the surgery. We next quickly confirmed that the other trap did indeed open into the third room, from which there again appeared to be no means of exit.

Then, suddenly, our investigations were interrupted by the sound of a heavy tread from the direction of the front of the house. Holmes smiled ruefully, saying, 'I should have secured the front door, Watson, for if I am not mistaken its open state has attracted the arm of the law. An unlikely occurrence in such an isolated locality. Just bad luck, I'm afraid, aside from my carelessness. I fear that we will have to declare our identity and purpose here.'

In confirmation of Holmes's words, a huge and burly police sergeant appeared. His ruddy face took on a somewhat guarded yet not altogether impolite expression, as did his broad country accent as he blew through his walrus moustache and asked, 'I suppose you gents have good reason to be here?'

We both smiled ingratiatingly as Holmes replied, 'Good afternoon, Sergeant. My name is Sherlock Holmes of Baker Street, London, and this is my friend, colleague and Boswell, Dr John Watson.'

The policeman grinned, saying, 'Oh yes, and I'm the prime minister! It so happens that I have a special interest in the exploits of Sherlock Holmes, I never miss reading of his adventures in *The Strand*. I have seen the photographs of him and in them he always wears a silk hat and morning suit or else a deerstalker with an Inverness cape and certainly not a tweed cap and torn Norfolk jacket.'

I tried to explain. 'Sergeant, the illustrations that you mention are not photographic but merely artists' impressions. I have seldom seen my friend wearing a deerstalker, and his cap and jacket are ideal for the autumn weather.'

At this the policeman grunted and asked if either of us had about us any means of formal identification. A search of my pockets produced nothing of use in that direction whilst Holmes's clothing was productive only of items of a seemingly incriminating nature. His notebook with the local names and addresses was taken by the sergeant to be a list of properties to be burgled, this view backed up by the discovery of the wire pick lock.

'Burgling tools, eh? Well, that settles it. I shall have to ask you both to accompany me to the police station.'

We were made to walk the two or so miles to Poolford police station, the sergeant walking behind us, wheeling and steering his bicycle with his right hand as he brandished a truncheon with his left. At least he spared us the indignity of handcuffs, though this may have been simply because he had none with him. I was thankful that our arrest had taken place in a rural area rather than, for example, in the East End of London, where our procession would have attracted a crowd of jeering louts!

Poolford police station itself proved to be minute as such establishments go. Just a front office with a desk, backed by a single cell of the old-fashioned type with a barred front. More like an animal enclosure from Regent's Park Zoo, its style though still commonly found in the United States was seldom encountered in this country, even at the time I speak of. Our particulars and circumstances of our arrest were noted in a huge book, partly from the sergeant's own notes and partly from the statements that we were both required to make. The charge was breaking and entering with a view to theft, and he sighed wearily when we still insisted our identities were genuine. He nodded grimly when I suggested that he should contact someone who might be able to identify us, but his expression changed to a broad grin once he had locked us into the cell. He asked, 'Well, mister detective, what do you make of your new apartment?'

Holmes glanced keenly around the cell, taking in its every detail before he replied, 'Well, I notice that it has seldom been used in quite a long time; it has not been repainted for several years and prisoners are not famous for their careful treatment of their surroundings. Notice, Watson, how the paint is in that stage of drying out which takes time to gain. However, there has been one recent occupant. An Irishman, at least six feet four inches tall, articulate, wearing a crucifix, and his crime very probably that of forgery.'

The sergeant's jaw all but hit the floor of the police station, until a gleam of comprehension came into his eyes. He gazed at Holmes through the bars and said, 'Oh, so you are a pal of Flannigan's are you? For a moment I thought you had done something clever.'

Holmes chuckled as he replied, 'I have never encountered Flannigan, to my knowledge, his name being the one detail which I could not give you. He has written a message upon the wall on the space just above the inside of this barred door. It reads, "Holy Mother of God, look upon me with compassion and return me to Erin. July 10th 1903". Beside this message there is a minute but beautifully executed sketch of the late queen, Victoria. A skilled artist and draughtsman, his most likely crime that of forgery.'

The sergeant scratched his head and said, 'That is all very well, but how could you tell about his height and his wearing of a crucifix?'

'Elementary, Sergeant. I have seldom met an Irishman who did not wear a crucifix, especially one who would write a plea to the Holy Mother. As for his height, I am more than six feet tall yet would have needed to have been about four inches taller to have written the message, there being nothing in the cell upon which he could have stood, for all the furnishing is bolted to the floor.'

I could see that a doubt was crossing the policeman's mind now as he asked, 'Who do you suggest that I should contact for purposes of identification?'

Holmes and I consulted and agreed, 'Inspector Lestrade of Scotland Yard!'

The sergeant grinned but agreed to do what he could. 'Very well, I'll try and reach him on this new-fangled telephone thing. I've only used it once before and a right performance it is I can tell you. Still, you can see what an up-to-date police station you are dealing with here. Had you done your burgling in Crawley and arrested there you would have had to wait ages while they sent a wire!'

The telephonic instrument was fixed to the wall and I must admit to have been somewhat surprised to see it in such a rural setting. The handle was turned and the sergeant spoke to the exchange in a voice raised to heights that suggested the telephone need scarcely be required. 'Hullo, this is Sergeant Bulstrode here, Poolford Police . . . I want Scotland Yard. That's right, you heard . . . Scotland Yard!'

He blew down the mouthpiece of the instrument and banged it against the wall. Then, for the next five minutes, he whistled Gilbert and Sullivan's policeman's chorus in a manner that must have greatly irritated whoever was on the other end of the telephone line. Then suddenly he spoke again in his specially loud telephone voice. 'Hullo, Scotland Yard? Bulstrode of Poolford here . . . yes, Sergeant

Bulstrode of Poolford police station. I want to speak to Inspector Lestrade. What? Yes, I know he's a busy man, my business with him is urgent. Very well, then, I'll wait . . .'

He glanced round at us importantly, then treated Scotland Yard to another verse or two of the policeman's chorus. After two or three minutes he suddenly stood to attention and saluted. 'Hullo, Inspector Lestrade? Bulstrode here, Poolford. I've got a couple of prisoners here, sir, who claim to be known by you. They claim to be Sherlock Holmes and Dr Watson and I'm holding them for breaking and entering. What do they look like? Nothing like the pictures in *The Strand*. One is tall, more than six feet, lean build, about fifty, thinning hair with a widow's peak, sharp features, well spoken but incisive voice. The other one is nearly as tall, military type, sturdy build, similar age, speaks like an army man, good head of hair, grey at the temples. Oh, I see . . . but you say that you do not want me to release them. Very well, sir!'

The sergeant saluted again and replaced the instrument upon its cradle. Then he turned to us. 'Sounds a bit strange to me. He says that he is pretty sure that you are who you say, but he doesn't want you released until he gets here. Says he wouldn't miss this for the world. Sorry gents, I've got my orders but at least I can get you a cup of tea.'

For the better part of two hours we waited for Lestrade to arrive. Holmes was philosophical, and having demanded the return of his pipe and pouch had soon filled the cell and the front office with acrid smoke. As he partly lay, partly sat upon the bed it was obvious to me that he was not wasting his time but rather was turning over in his mind all of that which we had learned since we had arrived at Reigate station.

When the inspector finally did arrive he was in a merry mood, laughing hugely at our predicament. He was, I was amazed to notice, accompanied by two men bearing photographic equipment. He said, 'Oh, strike me pink, Mr Holmes, Doctor. I'm sorry about this but I just had to see the two of you in the jug for myself! What is more, I just have to get a photograph of the two of you peering through the bars.'

Holmes took it very calmly, saying, 'Just as long as the picture is for your own private collection, I don't mind.'

We posed as the photographer exposed a plate or two whilst his colleague set light to celluloid collar stiffeners for illumination. Then, as we stepped out of the cell, I felt that I knew for the first time in my life what it must be like to be an apprehended criminal. Never again could I feel quite the same about a wrongdoer whose long stretch we had helped to ensure.

Lestrade at least had the decency to give us a lift back to Baker Street in his motor car, a machine of which he seemed extremely proud but profoundly ignorant. Every ten minutes or so the car came to a shuddering halt and the police driver would need to give it water, petrol, oil or treat it for some automobilic malady or other. We remarked upon how often the machine failed and were told that this was usual, even in an expensive police force Rolls-Royce. Holmes appeared to me to find this information thought-provoking. Eventually, talk turned to the activities in which we were involved. Lestrade listened politely to the version of events which Holmes chose to tell him. Whilst he expressed interest he insisted that he could not participate until some actual crime could be seen to have been committed. I felt that Sherlock Holmes was secretly relieved at this, perhaps preferring to follow his own star, as was his habit.

Back at 221B we found Professor Mainwaring seated by the fire. His face betrayed that he was still extremely agonised by his situation. Holmes greeted him warmly.

'Professor, we have much to tell you and whilst some of it troubles me still, I believe that I can see the light at the end of the tunnel. I believe that quite soon we will regain for you your wife, identity and status, not to mention your invention.'

The professor started, saying, 'The loss of my wife and my own identity had quite put such thoughts from my mind. I would of course be more than glad to regain my engine which would take me a long time to reconstruct, for I have no plan or diagram of it.'

Holmes said, 'Had you forgotten your finances, Professor? For having visited Lorrimer's Bank I have less confidence in regaining it than I have in my ability to solve your other problems. The account does not exist!'

Between us we told Mainwaring of our day's activities, skirting around the irritation of our arrest and incarceration. He said to Holmes, kindly, 'It is your turn to be in need of a good night's sleep, sir, after so much activity and thought process.'

But Holmes shook his head. 'As I grow older, Professor, I tend to need less sleep, very little in fact these days. Quite unlike Watson, who could sleep through an earthquake. Even when the game is afoot I usually have to rouse him roughly in the morning. I have invariably all but finished my breakfast before he puts in an appearance at the table.'

Mainwaring, who was clearly a kindly man, said, 'I used to suffer sleepless nights myself, especially when in the throes of creative activity. But Mary, bless her, used to insist upon giving me one of her tablets now and then. They were prescribed for her by Dr Royston and would make me sleep soundly . . .'

He rummaged in his pocket and triumphantly produced a small medical pill bottle, holding it up for us to see.

'By George, I have the very articles in my pocket and had forgotten them. Perhaps you might care to take one of them before you retire, Mr Holmes?'

Rather to my surprise Holmes took the bottle, peering keenly at it, and saying, 'Thank you, Professor, I may well try one of your pills later, as you say they were so beneficial to yourself. You took one on retiring?'

He shook his head. 'No. More often I would take one after luncheon whilst sitting with my wife before the fire. The combination of the one tablet and her dear presence would seem to produce the required soporific effect. I would sleep for an hour, sometimes two, and awaken, not just refreshed, but, how can I explain it, unburdened? Sometimes when I awoke I would fancy that I might have been speaking aloud, as in a nightmare. Yet there had been no bad dreams and Mary always assured me that I had made no sound, save those of restful breathing.'

Holmes, although I knew that he had been listening keenly to what Mainwaring had been saying, appeared a little preoccupied with a scanning of the pill bottle label. Then, to my great surprise, he appeared to change the subject. 'Professor, before I forget, there is something that I had meant to ask you before. The improved typewriter which you mentioned that you had produced. Did you have and use such an instrument yourself?'

Like myself I could see that Mainwaring found this change of subject a distraction. 'Why, yes. I was never able to sell the patent because some other inventor beat me to it. A case of great minds thinking alike, I suppose, so I kept the prototype for my own use. Mind you, Mary used it far more than I, for she handled all my affairs as I have told you.'

'Professor, you do not happen to have about you some example of work produced upon the machine?'

Mainwaring, though looking somewhat puzzled, began to search within his pockets, eventually producing a small piece of paper upon which some words had been typed. 'Here, sir, a list of materials which I had intended to give to Mary to order for me from a supplier. As you will see, it just mentions metal pipes and sheets of mild steel and the like. It is a trifle scruffy, I am afraid.'

Holmes took the paper easily, examined it and I thought I detected a gleam in his eyes. 'Thank you, Professor, for this and for the pills. Now I suggest that you return to your hotel for another good night's rest. I have some pondering to do, after which I hope too to enjoy an unusually good night's sleep.'

Once Mainwaring had left, Holmes stood the pill bottle upon the side table next to his chair, placing beside it the scrap of paper which bore the typing. He requested of me, 'Watson, would you be so kind as to pass my lens which lies upon a pile of newspaper cuttings? If I am not mistaken we have made quite a breakthrough.'

After peering at both items through the magnifying glass he grunted with satisfaction. 'It is just as I suspected, Watson. First examine the label on the pill bottle and as a medical man give me your comment upon it.'

I looked carefully at the bottle and its label, soon to perceive that it was not quite as it should have been. The label was a plain one without a printed heading from either physician or apothecary. There was simply a typed message, 'The tablets, Mrs M Mainwaring. One only or as directed'. I remarked upon its lack of credulity.

'Why, Holmes, no doctor nor yet chemist has ever handled or issued this label. It has been typed upon a plain white label and stuck on with glue by some person unqualified to do so.'

'Exactly, there is no printed heading or signature. It has

been stuck on, by the way, with office mucilage rather than glue, but you are otherwise correct. Now, I would like you to compare it with this typed list and tell me your findings.'

He passed me the paper which I also studied. 'The typefaces are both of a classic Roman alphabet but I see no other significant fact.'

'You mean that as the most popular typeface there is no coincidence? Look again at both examples through my lens.'

I studied both examples again through the glass but could find nothing to add to my statement. Holmes shook his head, chiding me sadly. 'You see, Watson, and yet you don't see! Does it not become obvious to you that both examples were typed upon the same machine? Notice all examples of the letter "e", or rather those of the lower case. You will see that the top portion has not been cleaned efficiently on all examples on both items.'

'Coincidence? It is after all the most used letter.'

'Very good, but study now the "l" and you will notice a small scar at its top, again identical wherever it appears on both items.'

He was right, as ever. Both examples of typing had been produced on the same machine and I hastily agreed that they had, lest he start to recommend me to yet another monograph. But I was still not entirely clear regarding the significance of the typing. He explained, 'This makes it clear that Mrs Mainwaring typed the pill label herself suggesting that she wished her husband to think that they had been prescribed for her. She gave them occasionally to him, and he told us that when he took one he invariably slept, or rather dozed, always in her presence. This is not only a minor breakthrough but makes Mrs Mainwaring herself a suspect, yet her abduction has been one of our main concerns. Was she abducted or did she go willingly and what was her motive concerning the tablets? Perhaps she wished him soundly asleep whilst certain events took place. There is a motive to it all you know, the purloining of his revolutionary air-machine engine. We have also established that the lady was taking his money to put into a non-existent bank account. He did not know of this or I'll wager many another suspect action because she handled all of his business, he being the classic absent-minded professor!'

Having spoken thus, Holmes went into a brown study from which I, from bitter experience, dared not stir him. But eventually he roused himself with a gleam of determination in his eye. 'Watson, I have considered the matter of the tablets deeply. To have them analysed would take time, which is not on our side, and the findings might not even tell us what is their exact effect. I have decided that I must become a human guinea-pig by taking one of the tablets myself.'

'Holmes! You cannot risk taking a tablet of which we have no real knowledge regarding either content or effect. Think of the risk . . .'

But he would have none of it. 'My dear fellow, we do know a little of its effect, it is soporific and we know it to be harmless for has not the professor himself taken one on a number of occasions?'

A fresh thought occurred to me. 'Have you considered that the tablets might be hallucinatory and responsible for everything that has happened or seemed to happen? I mean, could not the professor be suffering from hallucinations and not even be who he claims or believes himself to be? Perhaps this is the answer to the whole enigma'.

But I was clutching at straws, my concern for the well-being of my friend perhaps producing ingenuity of mind that was certainly not convincing enough to prevent his intention. He smiled at me kindly. 'Your concern for me does you credit, old friend, but you have forgotten the other clues to the mystery. The decampment of Saunders, Royston and the tenant of the Willows, the non-existent bank account. Mainwaring could not have imagined all these coincidences and they could not therefore be the result of hallucinations. No, my taking of one of these tablets may give a vital addition to our knowledge of the mystery.'

He removed the stopper from the pill bottle and tipped one of the small buff-coloured tablets onto his hand. Seeing that he was determined and that there was nothing I could do to prevent him in his resolve I handed him a glass of water that I had poured from the carafe. Then I crossed to the chair opposite to his as he swallowed the tablet, washing it down with the water. He then said, 'Watson, I will lay back in my chair and I will ask you to be witness to whatever may happen in the next hour or two. If I fall merely into a deep sleep do not attempt to awaken me, leaving me to wake naturally. There are writing materials to hand, pray make notes, oh and lock the door that we may not be disturbed . . . allow no in - inter . . . interruption . . .'

His voice trailed off and he was already drowsy. I locked the door and what occurred next was more startling and surprising than I could possibly have imagined or expected.

Interlude: 'The Amazing Confessions of Sherlock Holmes'

As Holmes's head rolled back onto the padded headrest of his chair I wondered just what to expect. In truth I rather expected that only sleep could result from his taking a tablet which had a history for producing a mainly soporific effect. Of course, there was risk and mystery involved due to the unofficial source of the medicine. My friend, however, was ever willing to chance everything for his cause, and I had to agree that the risk was a calculated one. In any case I was unable to dissuade him from his enterprise, which I watched keenly with great concern as well as interest, but I could hardly have been expected to predict that which next occurred.

Within two or three minutes of his ingesting the tablet, Holmes showed every sign of being sound asleep. The passage of a further five minutes produced a more shallow sleep during which he began to speak, yet still he slept. I followed his narrative alertly, though in re-telling it I confess that I must rely upon my memory to a great extent. I wrote down certain salient points, but could not record upon paper every word or even every phrase. The oration came in fits and starts but I resisted any temptation to interrupt, interrogate or prompt. So here, to the very best of my recollection, is what Holmes said.

'You will remember, my dear Watson, the account that I gave you back in '95 when I made a reappearance so startling as to cause you to faint for the first and only time in your life. Hardly surprising, for had I not been thought dead and gone, not only by yourself but by every other interested person in the world? It has then been lying heavily on my conscience, Watson, that the account I gave you at that time concerning my missing years was not an entirely accurate one. There were aspects of that period which I have always preferred to keep to myself until now. Mark you, there is nothing in the real story of which I need feel ashamed, and yet there are facts which might make you take a rather different view of your humble servant.'

Already I was intrigued, for Holmes had never, to my

recollection, been humble or in the least servile in his dealings with anyone!

'There are certain things taken for granted by the average mortal which have never claimed any part of my life; or so I have always led you to believe. With the passage of time I have started to feel that I should not keep anything from my only friend. Let me then start at the beginning. What I told you of my escape through clambering up the rock face and making my way to Florence was perfectly true. What happened thereafter differs somewhat from my official account. (The one I gave you.) Having reached that delightful city and having managed to elude my pursuers, at least for the time, I found myself dirty, injured, hungry and in grave danger of being discovered. As so often happens at a time when all seems lost, a stroke of good fortune presented itself. Thanks to a great deal of colourful publicity matter I could not help but be aware that *Aida* was playing at the opera house. I was not, of course, in a state of mind that would make me take any great interest in matters operatic or choral, Watson, but when I discovered from the posters that the principal performer was Irene Adler I became extremely interested. You will remember the lady, Watson, for she figured prominently in one of my earliest cases, back in 1888, which you later wrote and published in *The Strand* under the grandiose title, *A Scandal in Bohemia*. As I think you know, I have always held the lady in the very greatest of respectful regard; far more than I held for the client for whom we acted in the case. Moreover, I have always felt that, despite our being on opposite sides of the fence so to speak, Miss Adler had some respect for me. I believe I told you many years ago, Watson, that romantic thoughts or inclinations have played no part in my life. But Miss Adler, *the* woman, alone has made me ever wish that it could have been otherwise. Whilst I admired her face and figure, I above all admired her intellect and independence of spirit. Her marriage had, alas, been short-lived and she was again a star of the operatic theatre. I managed to reach the opera house certain in my mind that I had not been followed and I gained a place at her dressing-room door through affecting to have a message for Miss Adler from a famous American impresario. My firm knock was answered by her dresser who admitted me and bade me be seated. Madame, it seemed, was changing in the anteroom and would shortly join me.

'Some five minutes later, Irene herself emerged through the door from the extra apartment. No longer in her eastern exotica but wearing a cream tailored suit with matching hat and gloves she looked serene and even more beautiful than I remembered. The only sign that time had passed was that she showed the suspicion of a grey fleck here and there in her luxuriant hair. She looked enquiringly at me and said, "Good evening, sir, I understand that you have a message for me from Florenz Zeigfeld. From what I know of him he must think that I am a sea-lion or a juggler, for did he not promote the affairs of the strong man, Sandow?" I had risen; until now having held my head well down into my collar and neck cloth. Now I raised my head and smiled at her. "I believe you will recall our meeting some fifteen years ago when we crossed the most civilised of swords?" She looked keenly at me and, Watson, believe me when I say that she had still . . . or rather has still . . . a face that any man would die for. Do you remember the cabinet portrait of her that I kept at Baker Street? How often I had gazed at it during the years that had passed. She smiled and there was delight and mischief in her wonderful eyes. She walked towards me and placing a hand gently upon my arm said, "Mr Sherlock Holmes . . . I never dreamed that I would have the pleasure of seeing you again. Like half of the world's population I have followed your exploits in *The Strand.* How fare you, beloved enemy?"

'She turned a phrase neatly, Watson. Could it mean that she had felt for me thoughts that I had so secretly felt for her? I found myself addressing her in terms the like of which I had never employed before in my entire life.

' "Madame, though our meetings were fleeting and under opposing circumstances, no day has passed since when I have not thought about you."

' "Kindly, I trust?"

' "More than so, dear lady."

' "Call me Irene, and tell me more."

' "Alas, I am not a romantic, for my life has provided no time or place for romance. Had this not been so I would gladly have followed you to the ends of the earth!"

' "My dear Sherlock, you *have!*"

' "I will not deceive you, Irene, for I have turned to you at a time of great danger and trouble in my life. Only with great difficulty and good fortune have I managed to reach the sanctuary of your presence."

' "I understand; I would prefer that you had come to me because you could no longer resist my charms, but you may yet count on me as a friend in need."

'Although there was mockery in her tone I knew that she was a wonderful and very lovely woman . . . *the* woman, the only one there could ever have been for me. But I digress, Watson. I explained to her a little concerning the affair with Moriarty at the falls, my consequent predicament and present need to remain incognito. Her practicability quickly asserted itself and she sat me before her dressing-room mirror and with swift cool and deft fingers transformed my features with crêpe hair, spirit gum and dark powder. I soon looked more like an Italian mountaineer than a Baker Street detective. As you know, Watson, I have no small skill in the art of disguise myself, but I must give Miss Adler best. Finally, she produced a jacket belonging to a backstage worker and my transformation was complete.

'It was then felt safe for Irene to take me to her hotel where I was introduced to the reception clerk as Signor Castelli. She explained to him that my baggage would be arriving in the morning and requested that I be given a simple apartment. Then this enterprising angel took me to a tavern within the shadow of the hotel, where in a secluded alcove we took a late dinner. She nibbled a few delicacies whilst I made short work of a vast pile of spaghetti washed down with chianti and mugs of hot, strong, coffee. Then we discussed my future and the part that she could play in it. I tell you, Watson, the business in which I am presently engaged lost a promising participant when Miss Adler became a singer. Anything which she may lack concerning the powers of deduction she more than makes up for with her great practicality and active enthusiasm. She said, "Next week I depart for Paris where I am presenting a season. I can take you there as part of my entourage. If your disguise has held here you are unlikely to be followed to France, for your pursuers have no reason to connect us. Once you have reached the sanctuary of the French capital you can relax your disguise at least, or assume a new one more comfortable for you. If all goes well they will not look for you there."

'I agreed, adding that from Paris I would be able to wire Mycroft for money and set up a new persona for myself of a semi-permanent nature. This reminds me that Irene was very concerned regarding your good self. She was all but furious when I said that I would be forced to leave you in the belief that I was no more for quite some time. I assured her that some day, when I was able to resume my normal way of life, I would make amends. Alas, this I have scarcely done, have I, but rather have told you a pack of falsehoods concerning my lost years. The real facts embarrassed me and tempted me to invent fables. Tonight, however, apart from feeling extremely relaxed, I have felt an overwhelming compulsion to tell you the truth. But back to my story . . .

'I managed to keep to my hotel room whilst still in Florence, venturing out only at night. True to her word, Irene produced a suitcase containing suitable clothes and toilet items, telling the clerk, "Signor's baggage has arrived." I found that whilst the clothes were new she had managed to distress them in a manner which made them appear to have been used. Each night we dined at the tavern, undetected as far as I could tell. We held the most wonderful converse, on a high plane of intellectualism. Our talks were to me very dear and satisfying, yet never of a romantic nature, though our eyes met frequently and perhaps spoke more than our words. On the train it was easy enough for me to blend in with the other members of the *Aida* company. They believed me to be a local man, engaged on account of some specialised musical knowledge. My years of concert-going and tinkering upon my violin paid me dividends at this time, Watson, for I venture to boast that my conversation did not make me seem other than claimed. So on the train I passed into France with the rest of Irene Adler's company on the strength of her comprehensive permits. She was well known and loved in France and given the greatest of artistic freedom, which was as well for me.

'I parted from the company at the station and found a small hotel where I could rest, repair and lay plans. I wired Mycroft not just for money but for false papers which changed all, save my nationality. I had no further need of the trappings of disguise, but I did set about changing my appearance on a more permanent basis. It is amazing what a mane of hair and Dundreary whiskers can do. I swear, Watson, within a few weeks even you would not have recognised me. Irene and I had a final meal together in a bistro near the Opera. I felt more comfortable now without my crêpe hair and dark powder. Afterwards we said our farewells and her embrace was the first and perhaps only one of my life. She kissed me upon the cheek and said, "Dearest Sherlock, if only there had been a place in your life for me. But I understand, dear heart." '

For the first time ever I saw the gleam of a tear upon Holmes's cheek. But he recovered quickly and continued his narrative.

'Once back in England, Watson, I had to stand the indignity of watching the trial in which two of my most vindictive enemies were left at liberty. This meant that I had to bide my time and continue to conceal my true identity. I needed a new occupation, one that would not only enable me to remain incognito, but also give me freedom so that I could pounce upon my adversaries when the time was right, before recommencing my normal life. As you know, Mycroft kept the rooms on in Baker Street against that possibility. He was my only contact, my life-line, without whom I would have foundered. I could not, of course, set up as a consulting detective even under an assumed name lest similarity of methods might betray me. Now you have often referred to me as a mind-reader, Watson, and this put the idea of becoming just that into my head. Yes, as incredible as it may seem to you I went upon the music-hall stage as the Great Lomesh [Lomesh being an anagram of Holmes]. All I had to do was present a demonstration in which I used my deductive methods, without revealing them or the trains of thought which led to my conclusions. For example, some fellow would rise to his feet in the audience and shout, "You don't know me, guv, so why don't you tell us where I come from and what I do for a crust?"

'Well, the fellow would usually reveal his place of origin from the tone and dialect with which he spoke. If he was a Londoner I could even place him within a couple of streets. I would say, "You are from Hoxton, King Edward Street or very close to it. A plumber by trade, you are married and suffer the occasional bout of asthma. Recently you have been on a journey to the coast, where you resided for several days. Am I right?"

'I hardly need to tell you, Watson, how I knew these things; occupational characteristics, dialect, style of dress, wedding ring and a gasp for breath at the end of each phrase, plus an unnaturally pink complexion for a resident of Hoxton. The audience would gasp with amazement so that often I was tempted to tell them how it was done, but always resisted. There would be a rush of people defying me to tell them things about themselves that I could not possibly know. Later I would suggest that they pass artifacts to me which I would examine and then relate their history and that of their owners. Remember the affair of your late brother's watch, Watson? I appeared at variety theatres all over the British Isles, and managed not only to bide my time but to make a reasonable livelihood for several years. This style of activity might have been occupying me still had it not been for those events which you chronicled as *The Adventure of the Empty House*, bringing my theatrical career to the happiest of conclusions.'

His voice had started to tail off and he fell once more into a deeper sleep in which state he remained for quite an hour. When he eventually awoke he said, 'My dear Watson, I feel quite refreshed. Obviously I was on the wrong track when I took the tablet to be anything save a mild sedative.'

I told Holmes that on the contrary he had made a sensational series of confessions whilst under the influence of the drug. Still unconvinced that he had spoken the truth during these, I repeated what my notes and memory had captured from his narration. Rather to my surprise he shook his head. 'No, Watson, it was all perfectly true and I apologise for having misled you. But at that time I felt that the events as I presented them might be easier for you to accept, making life for both of us far simpler. However, as Shakespeare said, "Be sure your sins will find you out"!'

'Surely, Holmes, you could have trusted me with the truth, especially as your feelings for Irene Adler were already known to me. Love of one human being for another is nothing to be ashamed of.'

'When you are Sherlock Holmes there is no time or place in life for anything but the practical, the scientific, whilst following a trade which recognises only the actualities of life. We are wasting time with the discussion, Watson. Let us return to the matter of Professor Mainwaring and his invention.'

This was the first time that he had inferred that the revolutionary engine might play some part in the mystery. 'It becomes clear now that Mrs Mainwaring obtained information concerning the invention impossible for her to gain, save by outright enquiry. She possibly avoided this lest the enquiry should arouse suspicion, preferring to use the drug with which I have experimented, with such bizarre results. I suspect that she acted in league with others: Saunders, Royston and perhaps another. (Possibly he who claimed to be a long-standing occupier when Mainwaring attempted to regain admission to his home.) Something also that we have so far failed to consider, Watson, is where is Mainwaring's engine at this very moment?'

I confess that until that moment the engine had failed to impress me with its importance. Was this invention then the key to the mystery that we were investigating and the axis to a web-like wheel which revolved around it? Holmes appeared to think so, saying, 'We have wasted a great deal of time, Watson, and the trail could already be cold.'

I was willing to act at once, if the game was afoot, and if he would only give me some indication as to the form that our activity must take. But he shook his head. 'Watson, I have had my sleep but you will be useless to me if you do not get yours. I suggest therefore that we make the earliest possible start in the morning, commencing with a conference with friend Mainwaring.'

But my sleep was fitful and far from dreamless with my nightmare conjuring an image of the late Professor Moriarty falling from a cliff and clutching an engine to his bosom, whilst Holmes and the divine Irene watched from the cliff top. He was smoking a calabash and nodding dreamily as she delivered an aria from *Aida.'* It is said that dreams occupy but a moment of our subconscious thought. Certainly it was all too soon for me that I was aroused by a rough shake from Holmes.

He said, 'My dear fellow, it is already eight of the clock and I have sent word for Mainwaring to join us. Please be dressed and ready for anything within five minutes.'

I washed, shaved and dressed myself in record time, presenting myself to Holmes and the by then already present Mainwaring at the breakfast table within the allocated five minutes. We sat whilst Holmes and the professor played at eating and I disposed of my breakfast as we talked. I have always required a good meal inside me in order that I might face a day of activity, so I ate as I took part in the conference.

'Watson, I have brought the professor up to date concerning my soporific adventure of last evening.'

'Yes, Doctor, and what Mr Holmes has imparted has amazed and dismayed me. I am amazed that that which I took to be a mild sedative proved to be what it was, and dismayed that my wife, Mary, appears to have been in collusion with such subversive persons. I find it hard to believe. The only bright spot on the horizon is in that I could not have conveyed the true manner of the engine's advantages orally.'

Holmes said, 'Quite so, and I assume that they are unaware that they would need your presence to make its use clear?'

'Why, yes, although given a great deal of time they would eventually understand its innovation. Unfortunately it might take me as long or longer than that to construct another prototype. Time is not on our country's side, for the engine's possession by a foreign power might endanger its future. But what am I to do, for I cannot even prove that I exist, let alone take any steps to recover my invention.'

At these words Holmes handed an envelope to Mainwaring which he opened to discover a travel document made out in the professor's name, but giving his address as 221B Baker Street, London.

'Whilst you slept, Watson, my brother Mycroft, who you may remember at times *is* the British government, was roused. He in turn did quite a bit of rousing. Believe me, Professor Mainwaring, you have definitely recommenced your existence.'

Holmes was thoughtful as he said, 'If our quarry have got the engine they will surely want to get it across the Channel as quickly as possible. We will take an express train to Dover which seems the most likely port of their embarkation. I will telephone the port authorities to apprehend anyone trying to embark whilst in possession of an engine. With luck we might yet save the day.'

Our journey to Dover was uneventful as we were the only three occupants of a first-class smoker. But the time was not altogether wasted as it enabled Holmes to bring Mainwaring completely up to date regarding his findings and deductions.

Mycroft had done his work well and swiftly, for once we had reached the point of embarkation we were installed behind a partition which enabled us to study each embarking passenger as they passed the officials. Another observation point made it possible to view the passengers once they had passed and see them take ship.

I asked, 'Could they not take the boat train, Holmes?'

'Mycroft has it under observation, Watson, but I feel that this route is the most likely. A crated engine would be hard to explain away on a train and uncrated even more so. Large cargo items usually take this route and might normally pass through almost unremarked upon.'

We had to wait a long time before anything of pertinent interest occurred to us. During this long vigil Mainwaring not unnaturally plied Holmes with questions concerning those matters which he still did not quite understand. Holmes answered them concisely, though his eye seldom blinked as he continued to watch. 'Regretfully, Professor Mainwaring, all of my instincts and findings so far would indicate collusion between your wife and others to deprive you of your invention. In league with them she played a waiting game, the stakes being high enough to warrant even years of effort on their part. She tried to obtain from you and convey to them the secrets of the revolutionary engine in possibly a variety of ways. One that we know of was the use of a drug designed to extract details from your subconscious mind, which evidently did not work, probably because the information thus extracted was too technical to be understood. Eventually it was decided that the engine itself should be purloined. Saunders and Royston had already set themselves up with false credentials in the locality; the former as an estate agent without clients and the latter as a doctor without patients. Doubtless, Saunders had practised in the art of ridding himself of the few enquirers he got, whilst Royston set up as a doctor in an all but uninhabited district. Eventually you were lured to the so-called surgery where your wife and yourself were the only occupants. She went through the surgery door, giving you the impression that the doctor was in the room. Once inside she changed her appearance by means of theatrical disguise and a nurse's uniform. The deception gave the two men the opportunity to purloin your engine, probably using Saunders's motor car to transport it, and to effect the other changes to the Willows. Their object in this was not just the theft of your invention, but to drive you out of your mind, at least to the extent that your protestations would be disregarded by the authorities. With your finances also in their hands they considered that they had rendered you helpless. Fortunately, you had the presence of mind to contact me, and . . .'

Holmes's oration suddenly ceased and his eyes became slits as he peered through the arranged aperture. 'Quick, Watson, Mainwaring, look at the three people at the desk. I believe they are our quarry.'

Certainly one of the three was Saunders and a second man could have been the oaf who had barred Mainwaring from his home. (Although he admitted that he could not be sure of this as the man wore a soft hat pulled well down in front of his eyes.) The third member of the trio was a red-haired woman with thick pebble-lensed glasses. Mainwaring opined that with what he had been told and comparing her with the nurse at the surgery she could well be his wife, Mary Mainwaring. They had little luggage and no cargo, and were past the desk within a minute or so.

Transferring our attention to our second lookout position we were able to perceive Saunders, and those we took to be Mary Mainwaring and the so-called Dr Royston, clambering into Saunders's splendid motor car which was in position to be driven by way of a ramp onto the ship. I exclaimed, 'Holmes, could the crate containing the engine be already placed in the motor car?'

He shook his head, 'No, I alerted the authorities to search all vehicles and inform me of any such presence. We have drawn a blank and must now follow them to Calais in the hope that they will lead us to the engine. They must have managed to convey it, yet I know not how.'

We held a hasty conference and decided that the only useful thing to be done was to follow them to Calais and observe their actions. We had less than half an hour before us until the boat sailed, which meant some very swift preparations. The port authorities lent each of us a change of linen and other necessities, including travel bags. Holmes was careful to be sure that the bags did not match, and we made ourselves as inconspicuous as possible with the judicious use of hats and mufflers.

We kept well clear of our quarry, taking advantage when they repaired to the lower deck for refreshment to survey their splendid motor car. Mainwaring, the expert in such matters, declared that there was no possibility of concealment for a crated engine. Then from behind a lifeboat and in the shadow of a tarpaulin we watched our infamous quarry return and clamber back into the magnificent vehicle. The brilliant cliffs of Dover had disappeared on one horizon, signalling the imminent appearance of the French coastline.

After we had disembarked, we watched Saunders and

his companions with great interest, though from a considerable distance as their car was pushed down the gangplank and its mascot unscrewed to provide an aperture for the pouring of petrol from a can. Then Saunders spun the starting rod that activated the engine. They drove away, down the main cobbled street in an easterly direction.

At this point it would have seemed that all was lost, for it would not only have been difficult to find a motor car in which to follow them, but unwise to do so for another motorised vehicle would have stood out like a sore thumb. But a stroke of good fortune occurred when the vehicle, far from leaving our sight, pulled up outside a hotel (the Splendide) just a couple of hundred yards onwards. When they removed their baggage from the vehicle and took it into the hotel with them it became obvious that they intended to stay there, at least overnight. Pausing only to purchase some French cigarettes, Holmes led the way into an estaminet opposite the Splendide. Within the cool café we partook of refreshment as we sat and watched a minion of the Splendide drive the car into a yard. Holmes said nothing for perhaps ten minutes. In fact it was Mainwaring who broke the silence. 'What on earth have they done with it, Mr Holmes?'

My friend lit a Bisonte with a vesta, its black tobacco fizzing like a firework. 'I'm not sure, Professor, but I have a feeling that there is something here, something elementary, that I have overlooked.' He ordered a citron presse and said, 'Why don't you book us some rooms in this establishment, Watson, whilst I take a stroll and try to concentrate my mind. This may be a twenty-Bisonte problem! Come, I will see the two of you back here in an hour.'

Mainwaring and I tried to indulge in trivial chatter in order to rest our minds from the problems current, whilst Holmes was doing the very opposite, but of course our attention returned inevitably to that which had occupied us recently. We even tried to insinuate ourselves into a game, being indulged in by some locals in the estaminet; which seemed to be like a British game called shove-halfpenny. However, there were difficulties concerning language and temperament which precluded our inclusion!

It was in fact about half an hour before Holmes suddenly reappeared, wide eyed and all but shaking with some kind of excitement. 'Watson, Mainwaring, I think I have broken through the mist to some extent.' He all but hissed his words as he dragged us back to our secluded table. Once seated he seemed to very quickly become calm, and even insisted upon ordering refreshment before telling us of his discoveries. This had always been one of my friend's most irritating characteristics. He would grab one's attention and then play his cards with sloth. But after what seemed like an age he spoke. 'When I left you I took myself over to the space where the vehicles stood, to the rear of the Hotel Splendide. There, polishing Royston's motor car was a French lad with whom I soon became friendly. I offered him a cigarette and told him that I was a motor enthusiast from England. He pointed to the car and said, "This one runs like a dream, m'sieur; I noticed it when I was asked to drive it round here from the front of the building. I handle a lot of cars in my business as you can imagine, but I have never encountered an engine with such a purr!" This intrigued me and I asked if I could see this wondrous engine. He was good enough to lift one of the grilled side panels that I might see it for myself. Now my knowledge of machinery is not as great as it is concerning other matters . . . something that I must remedy . . . so one motor car engine looks to me very much like another. However, I could see that it was brand new, simply from its condition compared with that of the car and its other attachments, and with my lens I could even perceive that the screws used for the fitting were handmade. In these days of factory production this is a refinement almost entirely confined to inventors and other perfectionists. Mainwaring, I imagine that you make your own screws.'

The professor nodded and said, 'Old habits die hard, Mr Holmes.' The Baker Street detective continued his narrative. 'This fact and that of the bespoke nature of the engine led me to believe that it had been recently installed and was possibly originally intended for use in a quite different vehicle. This was rather borne out by the young lad's remarks concerning its unusual performance. Professor Mainwaring, I believe that your engine has been substituted for that originally used to drive Royston's motor car. This would account for the fact that we could not trace a crate connected with their entourage. Why take the trouble to find a way to smuggle such an unwieldy object when it would not be remarkable when put to its real purpose. Tell me, Mainwaring, forgive a layman's ignorance but could your engine in fact be used to drive a motor car?'

The professor had of course taken Holmes's point, saying, 'But certainly, though it would be extremely powerful and would take a little controlling.' Holmes, about to light another Bisonte changed his mind, and took instead a shortened clay from his pocket, which he filled and lit. I said, 'By Jove, Holmes, what an ingenious way of smuggling an engine!' I chuckled to myself. Holmes said, 'I should have seen through the ruse at once. It presented the only possibility, and you know my methods, Watson.'

We arranged for the hire of a gig from the owner of the estaminet with the provision that it should be ready to leave at a moment's notice. This cost Holmes dearly, but with the possible future of our country at stake money was not important; what had begun as an individual's own problem had billowed into one of possible international importance. We bade Mainwaring to get some sleep whilst he could, assuring him that Holmes and I were used to missing the odd night's slumber.

From our darkened bedroom we watched, Holmes and I, to make quite certain that Royston and his party could not leave their hotel without our knowledge. We observed in turn, with hourly watches until daybreak when we watched together and discussed the whole strange episode at length. I found it hard to reconcile the world importance that my friend seemed to connect to Mainwaring's engine and said, 'What advantage could a faster air-machine have to our enemies in time of war, which is waged with men, rifles, horses and cannon?'

'You are living in the past, Watson. Already the German forces have experimented with airships of the Zeppelin variety which could drop explosives upon our forces, our ships, yes, and even upon our cities!' I rounded warmly, 'Nonsense. Those great gas-filled objects are too large, slow and lack the mobility required to do as you say.' He replied, 'Watson, I pray that this may be so, though I doubt it. But in any case you destroy your own argument because the airplanes would have far more mobility. Oh yes, they may look like over-sized box kites at the present time but given ten years and Mainwaring's engine, who can say?' I said, 'Nonsense, they can fly at fifty feet for a few hundred yards; they would never be able to cross the good old English Channel!'

Later, the answer to my belief would clarify itself to me, but at that moment there was no time for Holmes to reply because he had detected the quarry leaving the august entrance of the Hotel Splendide. He hissed, 'Quick, Watson, the game is afoot. Fetch Mainwaring and let us hasten to the yard!' The professor was with us in less than a minute.

From the shadows of the estaminet we saw the motor car driven around the hotel by the young retainer. As he held the doors open for them, cranked the starting handle and then touched his cap they slipped a few sous into his outstretched palm. We watched the car take the coast road and were soon following in the gig at a rather more leisurely pace. It fell to my lot to drive the gig and this would have been an easier task had the cob not proved to be a little more than willing. As it was it was all I could do to hold her back lest she should bring us too close to our quarry. Holmes kept muttering, 'Hold her back, Watson' and 'Not too close, man', but eventually we managed a rate which kept the car in sight without creating suspicion.

It was Mainwaring who first noticed the temporary signs which appeared at the roadside. These were in the form of arrow-shaped boards bearing the words Fête Avion. He asked, 'Could it be that my engine is destined for an air display?' The thought seemed to interest Holmes greatly. He said, 'Perhaps we will very shortly discover if that is so, for I perceive that the motor car is slowing at what appears to be the entrance to this air fair.'

Flags of all nations were hung draped in a line to form a sort of welcoming archway through which a trickle of people were walking. A few vehicles were stationed upon the grassy roadside but we thought it prudent to stop the gig a hundred yards short of the entrance. We clambered out and reached the beflagged façade in time to see the motor car actually being allowed to enter the flying field on presentation of a document. The gate man touched his shacko and pointed, saying, 'Allemagne, à la bas!' We followed on foot to see the motor car driven into a hanger bearing a crest of the Imperial Eagle of the Austro-Hungarian Empire. In order to hold a conference we entered the refreshment tent where, over a glass or two of vin rouge, we tried to relax our tight nerves and make some plan for action.

'Watson, we need to know what is happening within the German hanger. Having given them a little time to busy themselves I shall send you in on some pretext or other, as an observer. They will throw you out of course but, hopefully, not until you have learned that which we wish to know.' I made some show at objection. 'What if they cut up rough?' But I knew that he would insist upon the plan. He said, 'Come, Watson, this from a veteran of the Afghanistan campaign? I'm a little too well known or I'd go in myself, and Mainwaring is very well known to them. In fact I'm going to give him my cap and scarf in case of a chance encounter.' He was right, of course. It was up to me as the most suitable candidate. Aside from which I was in any case the oldest member. In the event of any real trouble I had my service revolver and one Englishman is well able to handle a handful of foreigners! Half an hour later, assuming the most foolish and vacant expression that I could muster, I stumbled into the German hanger. It was not locked and inside there was a bustle of activity.

Three minutes later I was back in the refreshment tent, telling Holmes and Mainwaring what I had discovered. 'I walked in there like a bumpkin. I managed to have a jolly good look round before anyone accosted me, and had a clear view of mechanics who appeared to be installing an engine into an air-machine which all but filled the hanger. In one corner there stood Royston's car with its bonnet sides raised, revealing that its engine had been removed. Another, rather more used in appearance, was stationed upon the ground near the car. I caught no glimpse of either Royston or Saunders, but they could well have been standing behind the aircraft. However, I managed to take in what I have told you in a matter of seconds, which was just as well because I was almost immediately challenged by a mechanic who shouted at me in German and then in French as an afterthought. I comprehended the latter more easily, but it was clear anyway from his tone that he wanted me to leave, and quickly. I muttered an apology, having the presence of mind to do so in French, before hastily departing the hanger.'

Holmes nodded at me amiably and said, 'Good man, Watson. You have done well and I heartily approve of your strategic withdrawal. You allowed yourself to see that which we required to know without creating, despite your French accent, any great suspicion.'

Throughout my long association with Sherlock Holmes there have been a few occasions when he has praised some action of mine, but, as in this present case, the praise is always tempered by some tiny additional note of criticism!

Mainwaring asked me a great many questions of a technical nature concerning the air-machine but I was unable to answer most of them, having gained only a layman's glance at it. However, I was able to tell him that the word Voisin was stencilled upon it. That and an Imperial German eagle, other than which it seemed to have the box kite type appearance that I had seen before. The plane had looked to me like a mere skeleton, and anyone who attempted to fly in such a thing would be braver than I!

'So, they have fitted my engine to a Voisin? The French will not be exactly delighted, but suppose the Germans are at liberty to buy an aircaft from whomsoever they please during times of peace?'

At Holmes's suggestion we took a stroll around the fairground, keeping well behind groups of people wherever possible. With Holmes's cap and scarf Mainwaring was all but disguised anyway. We reviewed the line of stationary aircraft with interest, representative as they were of various makers and nations. The pilots stood beside their employers' machines, proudly answering questions from the crowd. The professor explained, 'When all the aircraft are lined up they will be turned around in rotation. You will notice that at present they are facing a cliff-edge which marks the northern perimeter of the field.' Doubtless, Holmes had already taken in these details, but for the first time I realised that we were hard onto the Channel. Eventually we were to see the big Voisin towed out of the German hanger to take its place in the line of aircraft, facing the cliff. We got as near to it as seemed politic to do so. Later we retreated again to the back of the crowd in order to converse concerning what we had seen. Holmes said, 'I deduce that the Voisin has been filled with petrol whereas the other planes have not.' About to ask how he had deduced this I halted before I spoke because the answer became obvious to me before I had asked the question. Holmes, ever the mind reader, tapped his prominent nose and nodded. 'Exactly, Watson, and I detected no such odour from the rest of the field. I assume then, Professor, that the planes are not really expected to fly.'

'I imagine not. They will doubtless be turned to show the public their propellers, and there will probably be a display by an entirely different craft, or even two or three.'

I asked the obvious question. 'Could it be that Reynolds and company intend to fly the Voisin, using your engine, Mainwaring, in an action completely unexpected by the organisers?' But it was Holmes who replied, 'Assuming the possibility of such an enterprise I consider it likely that our friends intend to fly the Voisin to the Fatherland!'

The professor whistled softly before he said, 'It would not be possible in one flight, Holmes, but they could make a series of hops, each of a few miles, assuming that they have staked out suitable landing fields.'

'You say a few miles . . . how many miles could the Voisin fly in one journey?'

'Normally just a mile or two, but fitted with my engine, possibly twelve or fifteen miles.'

It was Holmes's turn to whistle. He said, 'No wonder they are so keen to get hold of it.' I asked the obvious question, which seems to be my principal occupation. 'Why would they take such risk and trouble when they could have continued to drive the engine in the car, across the border and into German territory?' Holmes replied, 'Crossing the Franco-Prussian border is a rather different matter to landing the car at Calais. Every part of the car would have been examined with at least the outside chance of the new engine creating suspicion. Moreover, their scheme would be the perfect way to convey the Voisin into Germany without a lot of diplomatic difficulty. In short, they would be killing two birds with one stone. Once the plane is airborne we would have great difficulty in following it to its first scheduled landing. Come, we must evolve some plan and quickly too.'

Impatiently the Baker Street detective tore up his remaining Bisontes and crammed the resulting palmful of tobacco into a short clay which he took from his pocket. Lighting the resulting bowlful he created a cloud of pungent smoke, saying, 'Not much good, but better than they were as cigarettes. This would normally be a two- or three-pipe enigma, but I have neither time nor yet tobacco!' We were impatient, having no idea as to the direction that his train of thought could possibly take. After what seemed an age but was in fact only a few minutes, he spoke. 'Mainwaring, are you capable of flying one of these contraptions?' The professor replied, somewhat guardedly, 'Why . . . yes . . . I think I could fly the Voisin for example, especially as it is fitted with *my* engine.' Holmes nodded and asked, 'What would happen if you were to leap into the cockpit of the Voisin and take off, which I believe is the correct term?'

The professor considered and said, 'As it stands at present I would fly straight over the water, though of course I might be able to turn it if the winds are right.' Holmes, excited now, asked, 'But, man, if you were not to turn it, could you fly it across the Channel and land it in an English meadow?'

Mainwaring was, I could see, surprised, a little alarmed and yet secretly stimulated by what he was asked. 'I doubt it, I might make ten, twelve, even fifteen miles given great good luck. But the white cliffs of Dover are more than twenty miles away. I would land in the sea, well short of the target.' Holmes said, 'But the plane would float for a while and you would have every chance of rescue. More-over, the engine could be retrieved, could it not?' Main-waring nodded, saying, 'These things are possible. My engine has never been tested in flight, but yes, I feel sure that I could get most of the way across. I would need to take the engine somewhere for safe keeping, and I would need your help with the authorities.' Holmes replied, 'I cannot fly with you, but you would contact Mycroft Holmes at the Diogenes Club. He is familiar with the importance of the engine and can smooth all paths. Are you willing to give it a try?'

There was practically no hesitation before he replied, 'I'm game!' Holmes shook his hand, 'Good man! Now once you are in the cockpit what else needs to happen?' He said, 'Someone will need to throw the propeller, that's about all, except I imagine that our friends will need to be distracted, will they not?'

Holmes considered, 'I'm your man for the propeller because I have the muscular strength to do it. (Fencing and boxing, you know.) Watson will be able to do the distracting; as an old soldier he will be more than capable.' Mainwaring said, 'Holmes, Watson, you realise that there is a certain degree of risk involved for yourselves, too? To begin with the engine might refuse to turn and the three of us could be arrested. Even if the engine works perfectly I will not be the only one chancing his arm. The authorities will certainly detain you both.'

I said, 'Come, the French authorities, minions of a friendly nation, will soon realise the situation when we explain it and quickly release us.' Holmes's eyes twinkled, 'When you see Mycroft tell him that he may have to pull a few diplomatic strings.'

My heart was pounding a little as we walked towards the Voisin. Not from fear, you understand, but just from apprehension. Holmes was calm and Mainwaring seemed to be trying to suppress his excitement. The drill was that I would thoroughly distract Royston, Saunders and their pilot and try to hold their attention for perhaps a minute, luring them as far from the plane as possible. Holmes would give Mainwaring a leg up into the cockpit and then throw the propeller. Holmes gave me the signal and I ran up to the trio beside the aircraft shouting, 'Schweinhunds, Schweinhunds!' as loudly and in as ungentlemanly a manner as I could manage. Then I turned and ran about thirty feet away from them, next turning and pulling up some clumps of grass which I hurled at them without too much accuracy. They made as if to start towards me, hesitated, and I helped their decision by making unpleasant gestures and flinging more turf. This did the trick and they started towards me at a fair lick. I hared off towards the refreshment tent with the three of them in pursuit. My aim was to run around the tent hoping that they would do the same and not observe what was happening to the plane. The strategy worked and by the time they had caught up with me I was happy to see the Voisin actually airborne and on its way to the white cliffs of Dover! Saunders was the first to grab me but at that very moment he was distracted by the realisation that the Voisin was not only on the move but actually airborne. He turned away, making a completely useless pursuit of the plane in running towards the cliff. As his companions grabbed at my arms I could see that Saunders, having caught up with Holmes, had decided to vent his spite and rage upon the world's only consulting detective. Of course he was no match for Holmes, who was the finest boxer for his weight short of professional status, and was swiftly knocked to the ground. Ever the sportsman, Holmes stood smartly aside to observe if his antagonist would rise to signify that he was game to continue.

At this point a party of gendarmes arrived and both Holmes and I were arrested. Was it Andrew Ducrow who said, 'Cut the cackle and get to the horses? No matter who first said it, this is a phrase that I approve of so I will spare the patient reader a few of the finer details and recommence my narrative at the point where Holmes and I found ourselves answering questions at the local gendarmerie. The chief of police had absolved Royston and his party from all blame, despite our protestations. (They were, after all, official exhibitors.) We were charged with conspiring in the theft of an aircraft and starting an affray. In addition, and this was the unkindest cut of all, we were charged with impersonating well-known persons. After our experience with the local police in rural England we were becoming somewhat used to such accusations! We had nothing upon our persons to absolutely confirm our identities as all such documentation remained at the estaminet from which we had hired the gig. Mention of that establishment and the equipage only resulted in an added charge, stealing a horse and cart. We had a steadily growing list of criminal charges levelled against us.

Our request for Mycroft Holmes to be contacted at the Diogenes Club was refused and when we asked to see the British Ambassador we were laughed at immoderately. Taking my cue from Holmes, I said absolutely nothing about Mainwaring or his engine. (The Zanzig-style rapport of mental telepathy which Holmes and I had built up through the years told me that he believed that the story of the professor and his dilemma would not simply be disbelieved but would add to the complications of our plight.) The chief of police spoke at last.

'Gentlemen, you are evidently British but as far as I can see this is the only truth that we have managed to extract from you. You come to our country, you steal a horse and gig, and conspire with another person unknown to steal an air-machine, starting a fight with the owners of that contraption when they quite justifiably attempt to restrain you. Then for good measure you try to pass yourselves off as a celebrated detective and a respected medical man. Sherlock Holmes is a very different looking man from yourself, sir, wearing always the shacko for hunting the deer, the Scottish cape and smoking the large pipe of the meerschaum style. I have seen him many times on the cinematograph!'

Holmes chuckled, 'I am sure that it will make little difference, sir, if I tell you that I am impersonated in the shadow plays which you have seen by an actor, and quite without my permission. I rarely wear a deerstalker and Inverness cape, but an artist for *The Strand*, Mr Sydney Paget, appears to think that I do. Incidentally I have very catholic tastes regarding pipes and tobacco.'

It was useless, of course, and we were taken down a short flight of stairs to a cell within which we were left and lockcd. I suppose one would describe it as an apartment intended for temporary incarceration, its furnishing being of the most primitive imaginable, just a shelf which served as both bed and chair. It was dusk-like, once the solid iron door had been slammed shut and locked. But at least we were at last able to discuss our plight in private.

Holmes was thc first to speak. 'Really, Watson, had you not been truthful concerning our identities we might have been released with a caution for diplomatic reasons.' I reminded him warmly that we had been excused of implication in the theft of the Voisin and not just with affray. But he insisted, 'Even the theft charge might have been dropped as too difficult to prove. I blame you, Watson, for a good percentage of our present predicament.' I rounded on him, 'Really, Holmes. I quite fail to see . . .' He snapped back, 'Exactly! When you write your foolish accounts of my so-called adventures you contribute more and more to my inability to remain incognito. Until now I have counted as a blessing that Paget has produced the most passing likeness of myself, using his own brother as a model. Now even this blessing has turncd against me for I noticed a back issue of *The Strand* in the chief gendarme's office. Had the drawings resembled me we could have been bound by now for England, home and beauty! By the way, did you notice how Royston made sure that the officers saw the large number of billet de banque in his pocket book? At this stage I make no accusations, but will simply say that I trust our British police rather more.'

I was gravely concerned with what he said, especially with certain inferences. Holmes, I knew, was not a man to express pessimistic views of a situation unless it was well founded. I asked him, 'Do you believe that we might finish up as the prisoners of Royston and Saunders rather than simply of the authorities?'

'I feel sure that we will, Watson, the only blessing being that they might have difficulty in transporting us to the Fatherland as the border authorities would check our identities more thoroughly.'

'What do you think will happen?'

'To us? I believe that our friends will manage to take us somewhere for interrogation in the belief that we know far more than we do about Mainwaring's engine. They have lost the apparatus and its inventor, but they are enterprising people as we have seen from the scale of that deception which they organised in Reigate and its surrounds. I feel sure that they have been just as enterprising here in France. They are agents of the Kaiser and as such are just as ruthless and dangerous as their master.'

I protested, 'The Kaiser is a cousin of our own King!'

'Watson, a family feud can be of the worst kind.'

I was not made happy by his words and after what seemed like an age but was in fact no longer than half an hour by my hunter, we were again taken before the chief of police. He spoke to us as if we were children bent upon mischief.

'Gentlemen, through the kindness of Mr Royston and Mr Saunders you will be happy to learn that all charges against you have been dropped. I cannot prove that you conspired to steal the flying machine and the affray was, after all, a private fight. These gentlemen will take you to a private hotel where you can rest and reconsider your identities.'

All our protestations and objections were in vain. I even tried throwing an inkwell at the chief gendarme, feeling that we would be safer if we continued as *his* prisoners. But even though he was annoyed he decided to ignore the incident, backing away and saying, 'British high spirits, eh?' as we were marched off by Royston, Saunders and their driver (who later proved to be named Hauptman).

The gendarmes stood by to assist, should we have shown further reluctance to climb into the back of the big motor car which stood ready to receive us.

Once out of sight of the gendarmerie we could put up little more than token resistance. The pressure at my ribcage felt suspiciously like the muzzle of a revolver. We were both helpless prisoners. Probably for more than an hour we drove through wooded countryside until we arrived, evidently, at our destination. The car turned into a private drive and the outlook continued to be woodland. Eventually I caught sight of a discreet notice. I muttered enquiringly to Holmes, 'What does asylum mean in French?' He whispered, 'The same as it does in English.'

Eventually the vehicle came to a stop and we were frogmarched into the imposing entrance of a large mansion, evidently standing alone in thickly wooded countryside. A secluded retreat indeed.

Inside the entrance hall we were greeted by a thickset man with pebble spectacles which made his eyes appear much smaller than doubtless they were. He was wearing a white hospital coat. Royston spoke, 'Herr Freid, we have two guests for you. Both of them are suffering from delusions that they are well-known personages.' Freid enquired, 'Just who do they think they are?' Saunders answered, 'Sherlock Holmes, the celebrated Baker Street detective and his friend and colleague Dr John H Watson!' He spoke with heavy sarcasm and there was much merriment on the part of a number of white-coated aides who stood about. Two of them took each an arm of Holmes's and marched him away through an archway labelled East Wing. I could only exchange a helpless glance with him as I was in my turn propelled through another such egress labelled West

Wing. I was marched through a seemingly endless series of corridors, ultimately to be thrust into a room which was painted white throughout and furnished with a bed and a small cupboard beside it. Upon the cupboard stood a carafe of water and a glass tumbler. The door was shut sharply and I was alone in my white-lined prison.

I took stock. The apartment boasted no window, the sole illumination coming through a glass panel over the top of the door frame. My medical knowledge led me to believe that some sort of observation hole must exist, though I could not at first see it. But eventually I discovered that a patterned radial on the inside of the door concealed a slit. I discovered that it gave quite a good view in both directions when a small hinged cover was opened on the outside of the door. I discovered this through the rather unscientific prodding through the radial with a pencil. I opened the bedside cupboard to find that it had but a single shelf, bearing only a bible, printed in French. I poured a glass of water from the carafe into the glass tumbler. I took care to sip it gently lest it had been doctored. This was proved by a bitter taste to be the case. I considered that it was in all probability a soporific. I wondered how I could possibly manage without water, for if I were to spill it and demand more it was sure to be similarly doctored.

For a while I lay upon the bed and tried to formulate some sort of plan of action, imagining Holmes doing the same in a cell somewhere deep in the east wing. I consulted my hunter to find that it was almost four of the clock in the afternoon. I had been relieved of my revolver. Suddenly the door opened and an attendant entered bearing a small tray. He left this on the top of the bedside cupboard, grunting as he retreated. There was a dish of meat and vegetables, a cup of coffee and some fruit. The food, unlike the coffee, passed my taste test. I was particularly grateful for the fruit which quenched my thirst a little. I did not eat the meat as it was heavily salted, obviously a device to encourage me to drink the coffee and the water. These liquids I threw under the bed, hoping that evaporation would take care of them. At about seven of the clock I was visited by two attendants who marched me to a wash room where I was permitted to wash under supervision. Whilst throwing cold water onto my face with my hands I managed to swallow a good deal of it without seemingly being detected. In this way I managed well enough for two days.

Then at about noon on the third day I was taken to Herr Freid. He bade me be seated, his rubicund face wreathed in ingratiating smiles. 'Dr Watson, it may surprise you to know that I am very well aware of who you are. It is unfortunate that those foolish policemen did not believe you, you may think? No, it is fortunate for it has given us the chance to have a delightful conversation. I know all about the engine of the brilliant professor. We may not have it, but we do have *you* . . . you and your friend the meddler, Holmes! I have little doubt that you are familiar with many details of its construction which we would have learned, given the time to test it. If you were not mechanically as well as scientifically gifted Mainwaring would not be working with you, so no doubt you can convey all the details that I require.'

I replied, 'Well, I believe that the professor mentioned extra pistons and a new type of aluminium. Oh yes, and the screws are handmade, he actually makes the screws himself.'

The blissful innocent friendliness left his fleshy face. 'Doctor, you insult my intellect just as your pompous friend has done. I have excellent mechanical knowledge as I am quite sure you have too.' He glanced at me over the tops of his pebble spectacles and his eyes suddenly seemed four times larger. He continued, 'Oh, Doctor, what am I to do with you? You had better return to your room and contemplate. Tomorrow we will talk again, meanwhile I will have another encounter with your uncooperative friend. I have treated you kindly have I not, but I am afraid I can no longer endure Holmes's attitude.'

'Herr Freid, I have genuinely told you all that I know. Holmes knows little more, save that which his incredible intellect may tell him. I have laid all my cards upon the table and so, I am sure, has he.'

'How is the English expression, Doctor, you think I was very recently born, eh?'

I tried to convince him of my ignorance, of *our* ignorance, but I could not. He caused me to be returned to my pristine cell where I could only rack my brains and pray for some kind of divine inspiration.

For the twenty-four hours that followed, my regime continued as before. I felt no great thirst thanks to the illicit wash water and the occasional orange. I wondered if Freid realised that I was not getting the intake of soporific medicine that he had planned for me. He was no fool and I wondered if I would have done better to feign lassitude. Why he could not accept my lack of knowledge concerning the engine I could not understand. Did he imagine I was attempting to play some dangerous game of taunting or daring concealment of knowledge? I felt that perhaps I should be flattered if this was so.

On the following morning when I was taken before Freid again my spirits were lifted. It was he who played a foolish game. Before me on the table stood a kidney-shaped basin, containing a human ear. 'You see, your friend Holmes's lack of cooperation tried my patience too much. He paid for this with his left ear . . . if you do not tell me that which I wish to hear he will pay with his other hearing appendage.'

Herr Freid may have been a medical man, but his study, if it existed at all, had obviously been confined to a study of the human mind. Had he been a physician in the wider sense and had shared rooms with Sherlock Holmes for many years he would have known that no two persons' ears are alike, and that a man recognises those of a close friend. This particular ear had a lobe far thicker than it would have been had it been part of the stuff that Sherlock Holmes is made of. Moreover, the ear had been removed from its head at least a week earlier, and at a time when Holmes would have been safely in Baker Street. I decided that my best course was to allow him to believe that I had been deceived. With this in mind I gazed at the severed appendage in horror, and cried, 'My God, what have you done? You will pay for this, believe me! Do you honestly believe that if I knew more I would not tell you?'

He tried to conceal his unease and I felt that he all but believed me. Confused, he said, 'You know more than you have told me, so go back to your room and tomorrow I will present you with another portion of your friend.'

In the silence of my lonely apartment I sat upon the bed and racked my brain, trying to think like Sherlock Holmes. What would *he* do and what indeed was he doing, if anything? I re-examined the bedside cupboard for possible inspiration. I discovered that the shelf was not only easily removed but was constructed from three individual pieces of wood, tongued and grooved. I stood the shelf against the wall and applied pressure with a foot. Continued application of this action was eventually rewarded by a rending and splitting which would have dismayed any conscientious carpenter. I was presented with three pieces, rough at the edges, each about twenty-eight inches long, six inches wide and about an inch and a half thick. I took up one of them and formed it into a weapon by shaving a handle at one of its ends through scraping it against the sharpest metal edge that I could find on the bed. I brandished the resulting club proudly, feeling rather like Robinson Crusoe.

Having kicked the shavings under the bed I returned parts of the wood to the inside of the cupboard where at a glance they would pass for the shelf. Then I stationed myself behind the door, just out of sight range through the aperture, and waited for my gaoler's next visit. I passed the time making practice swipes with my weapon. I knew that I would have but one chance to fell the attendant and try to get out of the building. I prayed that he would come alone as he sometimes did. (Being a huge man, well able to take care of a lightly-built person such as I.)

I admit that the clink of the keys came sooner than I expected, at an unscheduled time, almost taking me by surprise, but I was well placed and with great determination I brought my homemade club down heavily upon the head of my white-clad visitor. He dropped like a felled ox, and a surge of excitement ran through me to be followed by one of uncertainty. Could I depend upon his lying inert long enough for me to make some sort of attempt at escape? Then another thought struck me; perhaps he had the key that would open Holmes's cell; if so, perhaps we could both escape, assuming that I could find the east wing undetected. I turned the fellow over with some difficulty only to discover to my dismay that I had beaten unconscious my friend . . . Sherlock Holmes!

Bewilderment gave place to enlightenment; Holmes, obviously, had taken the same kind of action as I had myself but his scheme had been a little further advanced than mine, in scope as well as time. I examined him quickly to discover that he was little more than stunned. Dipping my handkerchief in water from the carafe I revived him.

He rubbed his head ruefully, saying, 'What an energetic welcome, my dear Watson.'

There was no time for me to explain as he outlined his plan, 'Watson, I gave my attendant the same treatment that you meted out to me. Then I purloined his white coat and took his keys, intent upon rescuing you. Come, there is no time to spare, and if we meet anyone we can play the part of patient and guard and I will hopefully frogmarch you out of this dreadful place. But if we meet an enemy who recognises us both then we will have to throw caution to the winds and make a run for it. If we can gain the grounds our escape should be easier. As we walked together, I uncomfortably, along the corridor we ran into an orderly. Holmes propelled me along, roughly, shouting, 'Allez, allez vite!' Then he nodded to the orderly in passing.

Eventually we found a door which gave access to the grounds but it was unfortunately locked and responded to none of the keys which Holmes had purloined. But he managed to spring it with that portion of his penknife which I would have reserved for cleaning a pipe. Once outside we kept to the shadows encountering no one for some minutes, but eventually all but colliding with a roughly-clad man who apologised profusely. He spoke English and I was relieved to discover that he was a patient rather than an official. Holmes cast all caution to the winds. (Though if I had done it he would doubtless have remonstrated with me.) He said, 'My dear sir, I am Sherlock Holmes and this is my friend Dr Watson. If you could help us to leave this place you would be serving your country.' The fellow grinned and scratched his porcupine hair, saying, 'Sherlock Holmes, eh? Don't worry about it, mate. When I first came here I was Napoleon! Are you sure you want to leave?' We assured him that we did and he said, 'I can give you a bunk up, over the wall. It's only an eight-foot drop the other side onto soft ground. Do I get a reward?' Holmes, with great presence of mind, managed to swap the white coat for the fellow's tweed jacket, telling him that he had been promoted to the rank of an orderly. 'Herr Freid will be delighted!' The lunatic, pleased with his promotion, helped us over the wall at the place where he knew it was easiest, and our landing was a soft one, onto springy turf.

Our first vital need was for water, which we found, drinking from a tap no doubt intended for the use of gardeners. We ignored all medical advice on the subject, drinking deeply and unwisely and neither of us experienced any ill-effects later. Our next need was for a place of concealment where we could rest and lay some plans. We chose a nearby copse which gave us cover and a clear view of the asylum so that we could see anyone approach. We sank down gratefully upon the soft grass.

I asked, 'Holmes, do you consider that we are still in real danger?' He replied, 'Not if we are careful, Watson. I saw no sign of dogs in the asylum and without bloodhounds they would be hard put to find us in country like this. Once we have put ten miles between ourselves and this place we might even risk putting up at a farmhouse, or at least finding a meal somewhere.'

So we started out in good heart, eventually reaching a village where we were careful to remain on the outskirts. There we found a small café of the kind which sold fried fish and potatoes in a cone of newspaper, so that we were able to satisfy our hunger and continue to put distance between ourselves and the asylum. Fish and fried potatoes is a popular dish in France, though I doubt if it will ever become much in demand in England. But I admit that I have seldom enjoyed a meal such as that eaten from a cone of newspaper in a French woodland.

Our meal finished and by the light of the moon we

straightened out our cones of newspaper and glanced with interest at the first enlightenment from the outside world that we had seen for several days. It was Holmes who spotted the item which interested us greatly. He read it to me aloud in English, translating as he went along. It concerns an air-machine that had landed in a Kentish orchard!

APPLE PICKERS ASTONISHED!

In an orchard in Great Britain, not far from Dover, owned by farmer Joseph Hogg there yesterday occurred a most extraordinary incident. At about midday an air-machine descended having evidently flown in from a southerly direction. Like some vast box kite it gave the impression of having flown in from across the sea. This, however, could not have been so and our science correspondent assures us that such contrivances can only be flown for a few hundred yards at the most, so the possibility of it being of continental origin regarding its take-off is out of the question despite its German imperial eagle markings. The pilot was apprehended by the police and the area was roped off . . .

At this point the paper was torn and so Holmes could practise his French translation no further. I was the first to speak, 'Well, at least we know now that Mainwaring is safe and his engine too. Let us hope that the authorities will cooperate in contacting your brother.'

'Oh, I imagine they will, Watson. After all, the man has flown an air-machine across the English Channel, a feat undreamed of in aeronautics. Unless' (he indulged in some irony typical of him) 'they imagine that he has dropped from the Moon or Mars in the tradition of H G Wells! No, he and his unique invention will be in safe hands by now and Mycroft will liaise between the professor and the British government in general and the war office in particular. But as for ourselves, we are faced with the problem of getting back to England despite being wanted criminals and dangerous lunatics without funds or proof of identity.'

I asked, 'Could we not go back to the estaminet for our papers and other belongings?' But Holmes shook his head, 'No, Watson, there would be too great a risk of falling once more into the hands of that unpleasant and corrupt police official. We are quite on our own, my friend, and from this point on we had better be Smith and Carstairs.'

We slept out under the stars, and I slept more soundly than I had found possible on the asylum cot. I was awoken by a rough shake from Holmes.

'Watson, I have spent much time in thought whilst you have been snoring. Should we become parted we must agree to each make our own way home.' Reluctantly I agreed to his plan, seeing the wisdom in it, but little imagining that I would very soon be forced to follow it. We made the mistake of pressing our good fortune and brazenly put up at a secluded inn. It is possible that our lack of baggage and by now rough appearance created suspicion and that the patron himself sent for the gendarmes. We were in fact not long in our room and shaving with borrowed razors when the authorities, two gendarmes and Royston, burst into the room. He shouted, 'It is them, grab them quick, officers!' They grabbed Holmes who shouted to me, 'Quick, Watson, the window, and God speed!'

Remembering my promise I hesitated only a second before throwing myself through the open window, and landing upon the cobbles below with scarce more than a bruising. Like a hunted fox I looked desperately around for a means of escape. In fact, in my desperation, I leapt upon a bicycle which leant against the wall. Yes, I admit, I stole it, but it is theft I still consider justified in the light of later circumstances. By peddling madly I managed to be just clear of one of the gendarmes who emulated my leap from the inn window. He knew that he could not catch me on foot so he shouted furiously to some lads of the village who were just ahead of me. They made to impede my progress, but when they had taken a good look at me they backed away and let me pass, one of them even making the sign of the cross as he did so. I was evidently unclean in some way, though beyond my rough appearance I could not imagine in quite what manner. I cycled through a labyrinth of tiny side streets until I seemed to have quite lost my pursuers. I slowed down to regain a little breath and energy, only to have my uncleanliness explained to me. A villager looked at me, then ran away shouting, 'Attention . . . hydrophobia!' My fingers went to my face to come away covered in soap bubbles of a particularly effervescent quality. I must have looked for all the world like a man suffering from hydrophobia as a result of being bitten by a mad dog. I remembered that there had been such an outbreak in the area, common in those days and in that place. Foaming at the mouth was the dreaded sign to be wary of, but how were the peasants to know that the foam was caused by the application of shaving soap to my face. (After all, one does not often encounter a man with his face thus adorned in public, especially riding a bicycle.)

Just how fast, far or in which directions I peddled during the next hour or so I cannot be sure but can say accurately that I eventually arrived at a road signposted to Dieppe, though with no indication of just how far that town might be. But with the passing, and peddling, of another hour I arrived in what were clearly the outskirts of that delightful French coastal town. At this stage, having perceived no sign of pursuit, I was emboldened to stop and purchase a cheese roll and a glass of vin ordinaire with the last of my French money. Having consumed these I felt considerably better and almost optimistic. After all, my only problem was to reach my native land, a distance of little more than a score of miles away, even if across the Channel. This seemed a mere nothing beside the events that occurred during that adventure of *The Empty House* or those involved upon Dartmoor and its great slavering hound. However, I was quite alone, without the shrewd and enterprising Sherlock at my elbow. I abandoned the bicycle and made my way on foot to the waterfront. Without money or formal identification I realised that I could not buy myself a passage. I watched the comings and goings of sailors, passengers and others on the waterfront with keen interest. I noticed the officials who checked papers as persons walked up the various gangplanks. I moved about studying the situation at a variety of places. After quite a time I saw something which awakened a chord in my memory. It was a group of French peasants, dressed in cotton raiment, beretted and wheeling bicycles. Each of them had strings of onions hanging from their necks and shoulders as well as from convenient positions on their bicycles. Of course, they were the onion men from Brittany, a familiar sight throughout southern England. The Bretons would load up with onions and journey to the coast where they would wheel their bicycles onto boats and stand with these onion-draped velocepedes for the hour or so that it took to reach the English coast. There they would cycle the streets, knock on doors and sell their onions at a fraction of their English value. Once denuded of their stock they would wheel their bicycles onto another boat, and return to Boulogne, Dieppe, or whatever French port was available to them. Their stay in England would occupy only four or five hours and they would repeat the whole operation at least twice a week. They were honest, enterprising and hard-working men, and they provided me with an inspiration. If I could disguise myself as a Breton onion man I might be peddling a bicycle in Brighton or Hastings within an hour and a half!

I watched the line of bicycle-pushing onion sellers like a hawk. They trundled their vehicles and wares onto the deck of the cargo boat unaccosted. Evidently there had been provision made for a certain number of them in advance. All I had to do was replace one of them to get aboard. How? I could not quite see myself clubbing an onion man unconscious in order to steal his bicycle, onions and clothing. I moved down the neat line of vegetable-selling cyclists until I reached what at first appeared to be its end. But then, in the distance I espied another of them peddling like crazy and shouting. Evidently he was tardy and afraid of missing the boat. I thought quickly, for here was my opportunity.

I ran out in front of him and held up a hand. He stopped in bewilderment. I explained to him in my schoolboy French that I wanted to buy not only his entire stock of onions, but his bicycle and his clothing. At first he thought that I was mad, until he considered my British nationality. I had no money left, but I offered him my hunter complete with its gold chain, which he could see with his shrewd peasant eyes was worth a couple of dozen expeditions to the south coast of England. In a side alley we exchanged outer garments, and within minutes I was peddling towards the retreating line of onion men.

'Allez vite!' The French official made a final tick on his list and waved me onto the deck. His list tallied and I was on my way to England, so everyone was satisfied. Mark you, dear reader, I had to do a lot of grunting and shrugging during the next hour and a half in order not to betray my true-blue British identity!

I had no idea where the cargo ship would arrive at, for these craft plied between innumerable routes. I had hazarded a guess that it might be Newhaven, but I had guessed wrong. I realised when we came into a harbour in miniature which I recognised as that of Shoreham, a village between Worthing and Brighton. Wheeling my bicycle load of onions down the gangplank at Shoreham Harbour was easier even than had been the reverse operation. Soon my fellow onion men were off on their metal steeds, in search of prosperous leafy suburbs, leaving me standing with my wares in Shoreham High Street.

'Now then, Froggy, on your way. I don't mind you a knocking on doors but don't you try and sell your wares here in the street.' The portly policeman was a welcome sight and I tried to tell him my story, 'Constable, I am not French, I am an English doctor, friend and colleague of Sherlock Holmes. It is vital for me to contact certain important personages on a matter of national importance.' The policeman pushed back his helmet and blew gently through his walrus moustache. He said, 'Upon my word, you've learned to speak just like an English gent, you have. Even so, Pierre, or whatever your real name is, you can't fool me. Now go about your business or I'll arrest you.'

I had not had the best of luck with the authorities of late, so I decided to take his advice. I went to the railway station and tried to obtain a ticket to Victoria Station, which I knew I could reach via Brighton. I offered vast quantities of onions in exchange for a single ticket to London but to no avail. I began slowly to realise that I had fallen out of the frying pan and into the fire. I could have sat down in the street and wept, but instead I decided to show my initiative.

'Onions, lovely Breton onions, very, very sheep!'

I went from door to door, offering the onions at a fraction of their value and soon realised how hard is the life of an onion man. But in time I had sold enough onions to buy a train ticket. Then throwing caution to the winds I sold the rest of the onions to a café proprietor for next to nothing and the bicycle to a junk dealer for ten shillings. Happily rid of all encumbrances I walked into an inn called the Eight Bells and Bowling Green and demanded a tankard of ale. At first the innkeeper did not wish to serve me, saying that he was not fond of 'Froggies', but a kindly fisherman stood in my corner and even stood me a pork pie. Experience had shown me that I must follow the path that fate had carved for me, so I assumed a French accent in thanking the fisherman who told me he was 'Captain Page, but round 'ere they calls me Fairy, on account of the little folk.' I decided not to tell Fairy any of my troubles, preferring to enjoy his friendly company. I felt that any truthful account of my adventures would ruin our evening!

An onion man without his onions is someone to be stared at and commented upon, at least on the Brighton to Victoria train. Worse was to come when I attempted to hire a hansom to take me to Baker Street. Eventually I travelled there on the top deck of an omnibus, being refused admission to the lower one. I had decided to go straight to the rooms rather than to risk making a scene at the Diogenes Club in my onion man's outfit. Only one hurdle remained between myself and a hot meal, a bath and a comfortable bed . . . Mrs Hudson. She shouted at me on the doorstep, 'No, don't want any onions, shove off!'

I replied to the effect that I had no onions, which was the truth. She looked around suspiciously for a bicycle and wares, then a little puzzled asked, 'Well, if you haven't got any onions, what on earth are you wasting my time for?' She knew a Breton onion man when she saw one, onions or no onions. I removed the beret and smiled ingratiatingly. At last she recognised me and pulled me urgently inside, shutting the front door and saying, 'What will the neighbours think?' I reminded her of the motley crew that had often constituted Holmes's clientele.

On the following morning I took an early (for me) breakfast and informed Mrs Hudson with a somewhat curtailed version of our adventures. She was very concerned, as I was myself, concerning the welfare of Sherlock Holmes, but said, 'I'm sure Mr Mycroft will know what to do.'

In the sepulchral atmosphere of the Diogenes Club I was almost tempted to cry out at the sight not only of Mycroft Holmes but that of none other than Professor Mainwaring. As it was, my startled gurgle, the result of restraining a loud cry, resulted in a number of members lowering their newspapers and making tut-tutting noises. I shook hands with Mycroft and Mainwaring and the next few minutes was spent with my listening to the professor's narrative concerning his experiences of the period since I had last seen him. He said, 'Doctor, thanks to yourself and Mr Holmes, I did, as you know, manage to get the machine airborne. In making for the English coast I had expected to fall well short of that target hoping to land safely in the sea, near enough to make rescue practical. I am not a strong swimmer so you can imagine my delight when the engine behaved even better than I could have dared to hope for. It really was beyond my wildest dreams to land on Kentish soil . . .'

Mycroft interrupted at this point, saying, 'Watson, Mainwaring's engine is quite revolutionary and is already in the hands of the correct authorities with the war office. But we must keep all of this business quiet. The yokels in the orchard are not too bright and have been told that the plane started out from a quite nearby place. Even journalists are wary of believing otherwise, fortunately. The world at large must *not* know that we can fly the Channel. If we are able to keep this information and invention under cover, imagine the immense advantage we would have, should, God forbid, a war break out between ourselves and any of the European countries. I tell you, a force of planes equipped with Mainwaring's engine would make us quite invincible.'

To be truthful I was rather more concerned at that moment in time with the fate of my friend, his brother Sherlock Holmes, and said as much. Neither Mycroft nor Mainwaring had heard of the adventures which Holmes and I had endured and I attempted to commence a narrative. Then it was that Mycroft uttered words which all but made me endow him with psychic powers.

'You were about to tell me, my dear Watson, that once Mainwaring was safely in the air you were both apprehended by the foreign agents, aided by the local French police. Did you tell them who you were?'

'Why, yes, we did.'

'So, you did, but you were not believed and finished up, the pair of you, in an asylum for lunatics.'

'How could you possibly know that?'

'My dear fellow, if a sneak thief pinched my watch and then told the police that he was the Archbishop of Canterbury, and appeared to mean it, would he not finish up in such an establishment. Was it an official or private hospital?'

'It was a private establishment.'

'Quite, and suggested, I'll be bound, by the agents Royston and Saunders. But you managed to escape, otherwise you would not be standing here now. You were deprived of water, but since then have consumed quite a large quantity of red wine.'

I started. 'Good Lord, I know quite a deal about your brother's methods, but . . .'

He interrupted, 'Sherlock's methods are quite elementary in comparison with my own. Red wine produces a certain shade of ruddiness in the complexion if taken in quantity by a person who has been dehydrated. You journeyed to the coast on a bicycle, and crossed the Channel in disguise.'

'How did you know about the bicycle?'

'My dear chap, when you sat down and crossed your legs I observed the sole of your right boot, evidently the only part of your clothing which has shared your adventures and is worn by you at this moment. You will observe, Mainwaring, that mark, edged by a more distinct groove produced by the metal pedal edging? Oh, and Watson, you crossed the Channel in disguise as I said.'

I played my trump card, 'Ah, but *what* was my disguise?'

'You got yourself up as a Breton onion man!'

I could not believe that he had deduced this fact, and suspected some sort of trickery. I said, 'There is no way you could have learned that unless you have been informed by some observer, perhaps the policeman at Shoreham?'

'No, Watson, you have lost weight not unnaturally during your escapades, indeed your collar seems large enough for you to be impersonating a tortoise. Portions of your neck are visible to me. There are indentations caused, I deduce, from many hours of contact with those strings of onions which are brought here from Brittany. Notice, Mainwaring, the fibre marks which are unmistakable. But I am more concerned now that you are safe to learn all you can tell me concerning the fate of Sherlock.'

I told him of our parting when I leapt from the window. 'Royston was there with two local gendarmes.'

'Anyone from the asylum?'

'Why no, and Holmes, if he is still with the police, will have claimed Smith as his name.'

'What was the name of the village?'

'It was Ville-Aesop.'

Mycroft Holmes rang for a messenger and then scribbled a note upon Diogenes Club notepaper with a gold fountain pen. His plump, delicate hand making quick work of the task. He said, 'Do not worry, Watson. Holmes will be back with us by midnight, or tomorrow morning at the latest.' I put my foot in it by saying, 'But surely with so much red tape involved only the government could pull such strings?'

He looked pityingly at me and said, 'My dear Watson, there are times when I *am* the government, and this happens to be one of those times!'

'It has been a pleasant enough day, Watson, has it not?'

It was midnight at the Baker Street rooms. I had heard the sounds made by a hansom cab arriving but could hardly have expected it to be bringing Baker Street's most celebrated resident back home. 'Holmes, thank heaven you are safe. How did you get here so quickly?'

Irritatingly, Holmes insisted on seating himself and arousing the faithful housekeeper to bring him hot coffee. Mrs Hudson was delighted. 'Mr Holmes, it is a pleasure to set eyes upon you again . . . things just have not been the same without you.' Holmes glanced around him and replied, 'I can see that . . . the room is depressingly neat!' Even more irritating was his insistence on hearing my story before he would relate his own escapades. He settled comfortably in his armchair and revelled in the availability of his pipes and tobacco. Within a few minutes you could have cut the atmosphere with a knife, as of yore, so the good housekeeper's efforts in the direction of air purity were all for nothing. But then, it was good to see his sharp features again, peering at me through a blue fog. It took me half an hour to tell him my story which I could have related in ten minutes but for his constant interruptions in the shape of piercing questions. He was greatly amused by my adventures as a Breton onion pedlar and he laughed heartily and long, which is rare with him. When he had recovered sufficiently to speak, he said, 'Upon my word, Watson, you are an enterprising fellow to be sure. It is always good to have a sideline that you can depend upon. When patients are thin upon the ground I can just picture you scurrying off to Britanny for another load of onions! Now I believe you might like to hear of my own adventures? Very well, but I warn you they are nowhere near as entertaining as your own. After your spectacular leap through the window, I was of course taken, manacled, to the local gendarmerie. I claimed to be British, which was correct and that my name was Smith, which of course was not. But I soon realised that the police chief at Ville-Aesop was a rather different sort of man to his counterpart who had landed you and me in a madhouse. Saunders brought up, unwisely for him, as it transpired, my earlier claim to be Sherlock Holmes. He did so not for any other reason than to regain my person for transportation to his convenient private lunatic asylum. But this was not granted to him by the canny official. I could see, through my long study of human nature, that there was some doubt in his mind concerning my real identity. I preferred to remain safe with my Smith alias. I was incarcerated in a cell, but my treatment was a good deal better than that which we experienced earlier. I was given an excellent meal and even wine and treated with civility by the gaolers. It seemed to me that the gendarmes were trying to safeguard their conduct just in case I should turn out to be a well-known personality. Even so, I stayed my hand from playing any sort of Sherlockian card. After an hour or so I was taken to the office of the police chief. He was extremely polite to me as before, saying, "My dear sir, I see no reason to keep you imprisoned when my only duty is to detain you. Once again I ask for your name and nationality." I replied, "Smith, British." He said, "I see, and you make no comment upon the accusation that you tried to impersonate the famous detective Sherlock Holmes?"

' "Sir, I am not guilty of any sort of impersonation."

' "Not even of impersonating someone called Smith?"

' "I would prefer not to make any comment."

'He considered before saying, "Look here I appreciate that if you are indeed Sherlock Holmes you may be trying to avoid admitting it lest I at once assume that you are troubled in your mind and imagining this identity, as Mr Royston claims. For the moment I will not press you further upon the question of your identity, but may I suggest that you accompany one of my officers upon his rounds . . . shall we say . . . just to pass your time?" I agreed to do so, suspecting that which was in his mind. And so it was that I found myself handcuffed and in a police vehicle, rather like a dog-cart, driven by one Sergeant Chevalier. He spoke good English and was not only as polite as his superior but actually genial in his manner towards me. As he drove, he said, "My dear sir, if you are who I suspect you to be, you might find our next activities somewhat pedestrian. We have few murderers or international forgers in Ville-Aesop."

'Our first stop was at a small jewellery shop where there seemed to be quite a lot of activity. Two prisoners stood within the shop, held by gendarmes. One of them was a ferret-faced, wiry individual of some five and twenty years. The other was perhaps ten years older, a plumpish man, and both were dressed in a manner typical of that region. Chevalier questioned them both in a keen, professional manner. He also questioned the patron of the shop, a short, dark-haired man in a black-tailed coat and neat striped trousers, razor-creased and culminating in spatted shoes with somewhat pointed toes. The patron and the gendarmes explained the situation. There had been a robbery from the strongroom of the shop, the door to which we could see behind the counter. A quantity of jewellery had been stolen, mainly from a single packing case in which there remained a number of small pieces of lesser value than those which had been taken. Those that remained lay amid some straw-chaff packing material at the bottom of the box. The door had not been forced and the only possible way into the apartment had been through a high window of quite small dimensions. Needless to say, the window had been barred on the inside, but the barred frame lay upon the floor and the window glass had not been broken. The thief had most easily forced the window which was not very strongly secured in the, as it happened, mistaken belief that the bars inside it would make entry impossible. The gendarmes explained to Chevalier that the two suspects being held had both been seen, though not together, in the vicinity of the window at a late hour on the previous night. They both seemed, as local bad characters, to be likely for the role of perpetrator of the theft.

'I drew Sergeant Chevalier aside and pointed out that the screws had been removed from the barred frame, the holes enlarged and the whole thing replaced, possibly some considerable time prior to the incident. This indicated a confederate on the inside. He asked me, "Which of the two suspects do you consider most likely to have made the actual theft?" Really, Watson. Had you been there you would have agreed that the choice was elementary. I said, "The older of the two is completely eliminated, his build would preclude his entry through the window, however easily the bars could be removed." Chevalier smiled and nodded, saying, "Exactly, but can we prove that he was the thief?" I said, "We can try."

'Back in the front of the shop, Chevalier explained to the patron and both suspects that I was a consultant on certain kinds of crime. He excused my manacled wrists by saying that I was testing the new regulation handcuffs. If they believed him I cannot say. He moved the thin-faced suspect to one side and started to question him regarding his movements of the previous night and evening. I was not too interested in this, having already thought him the premier candidate for the robbery. I studied his clothing. He wore the currently fashionable pea jacket with some rough tweed trousers, the bottoms of which were, I noted, turned up in the style made fashionable by our own King Edward. With Chevalier's permission I asked the man a few questions, such as had he been wearing the same clothes as now on the previous evening, and a few more to lull his suspicions. He said yes to everything. I then suggested to Chevalier that he should search the fellow's clothing, even the most seemingly innocent of areas. In the temporary turn-ups of his trousers we found what I was looking for, a small amount of the straw chaff in which the jewellery box had been partly filled. Chevalier signed to a gendarme to take the suspect away. As soon as I had indicated the chaff he had understood perfectly what was in my mind.

'I said to him, quietly, that we were but halfway home. "We have the actual thief but not the confederate who made it all possible." We ruled out the probability, though not the possibility, of the patron having conspired to rob his own shop. (After all, Watson, such things have happened where the goods have been heavily insured against theft.) But we questioned him carefully, especially concerning all possible access to the strongroom. He told us that only he and his single assistant had ever had recent access to the room. When I asked of the various movements of his assistant upon the previous evening he told me that Isadore Levi, for that was his name, had not been in the shop at the time when he had closed it. I did not need to ask him why, for the name indicated the Jewish faith or at least its likelihood. The previous day had been, of course, the eve of the Jewish sabbath. Moreover, we were told that Levi would not be expected for a day or two as his mother had died, which involved various rituals. I asked, "When did Levi tell you of this?" He said, "Why earlier yesterday. He is an Orthodox Jew, never works on the Saturday anyway, and seemed grief stricken." I enquired, "But aside from his grief how did he appear?" He responded, "Otherwise as usual, extremely neat in appearance." He had not mentioned the one fact that now interested me. "Was he as neatly shaven as usual?" "Why yes, he has a dark beard but it is always very closely shorn." I turned to Chevalier saying, "Sergeant, I believe that if you can catch Isadore Levi you have your man. No Orthodox Jew would shave so soon after the death of his mother, so the bereavement is an excuse, and he may be secure in not being suspected for a while. You may yet be in time!"

'As it turned out, Watson, my deductions proved correct in all details and Levi was arrested in the very act of absconding with enough precious stones to make him a rich man for life. The narrow-faced man proved to be his accomplice and his confession helped to conclude the whole matter. In any case, Chevalier was convinced as to my real identity and said as much to the already half-convinced chief of police. But would you believe it, the whole escapade was of no importance, at least to me, because even as I started to take the gendarmerie into my confidence and confess my real identity the long-awaited messenger from the ambassador arrived. Mycroft's string-pulling had worked.

'So, Watson, I was given a change of clothing, long overdue for I had noted how the others were beginning to seek the windward of me. I was taken, in custody but protective this time, to the boat-train and travelled thence to Victoria Station. The rest you know, except that you may not be aware that we are both still considered to be in danger from enemies of our country, which explains the presence of the men from Scotland Yard.'

He indicated two bowler-hatted gentlemen in the street below. From the window I could see that they were plain-clothes detectives, but hoped that an enemy might not find them quite so obvious. On the following morning we were still at breakfast, enjoying those traditional dishes which one can so easily learn to take for granted, when a messenger arrived with a note from Mycroft to the effect that we should accompany the bearer to an undisclosed location. We dressed in tweeds and caps, feeling that an out-of-town destination was probable. A hansom was drawn up outside for our use and inside that vehicle we discovered a presence which should have cured any doubts we might have harboured concerning the authenticity of the message (for it had crossed my mind that we might be abducted again by our enemies) for there sat Inspector Lestrade of Scotland Yard. He touched his hat and said, 'Mr Holmes, Doctor, the war minister considers that this here engine business be placed in proper experienced hands. I have been assigned to make sure that the invention, its inventor and your good selves are fully protected.'

Holmes grinned at me as he said, 'I'm sure we can all heave a sigh of relief now that you are in charge, Inspector.' I coughed to disguise an involuntary chuckle.

Our rendezvous proved to be a very large building of a

somewhat temporary nature and situated in open country. We were not supposed to know its exact location, but I believed that Holmes had kept track of exactly where we were going, despite many twists and turns in our journey. It evidently was a place for the testing and perfection of weapons of defence and offence, for we passed a firing range on our way from the hansom to the building's entrance. Inside we were greeted by a British army colonel who led us to an apartment where we found not only Professor Mainwaring, but his revolutionary engine as well!

Mainwaring was delighted to see us and said, 'Gentlemen, it is so good to see you *both* again, especially yourself, Mr Holmes, for I knew that the good doctor was safe.' Holmes and the professor exchanged stories of the events that had occupied them since that dramatic moment when the Voisin had taken off and flown to Kent against all odds. The colonel began to betray a certain amount of impatience, so we all gave him our undivided attention. Colonel Faversham said, 'Now see here, chaps, this jolly old invention of Mainwaring's has been given preliminary tests and shortly it will be fitted to one of our new flying machines to have a proper test flight. Now you already know what it has done in flying the jolly old Channel, what? Well, I have to tell you that the whole thing has got to be kept a complete bally secret. Can't have the Huns or the Frogs knowing all about it, what, or at least no more than they already unfortunately do. I don't believe, after consultation with young Mainwaring here, that they have learned enough to be able to duplicate it. They may not even know that it actually flew the Channel, so mum's the word, eh?'

Mainwaring said, 'From what they have learned it will in any case take them several years to even begin to produce an engine like it. Rest assured that I have kept my silence, and I am at this time working on another invention which, combined with the engine, could make our country invincible in time of war. I intend to stay here until all is perfected, as I do not wish further adventures of the kind I have experienced.'

As we left the experimental engine-testing room I gained the impression that Holmes was growing bored with the whole episode. He had solved the problem of Mainwaring's lost identity and had played a principal part in restoring the engine to those with whom it should be. He wondered why his services should be any longer required. At least, from long acquaintance I believed that he felt that way. Also, I had several times noticed a steely glint in Holmes's keen eyes whenever the words 'invincible in war' had been spoken. I confess that whilst as patriotic as the next man (for did I not make my own small contribution to the building of the British Empire?) at the same time I felt slightly uncomfortable about the possibility of a secret weapon. But then, of course, one had to consider how much more dangerous such a device would be in the hands of those with less scruples than those held by the ministers of King Edward.

We started towards the entrance, Holmes, myself and Lestrade, and had all but reached it when a young man in a white laboratory coat ran after us in what can only be described as a highly agitated state. His voice had an urgency that told of his feelings of horrified shock. Yet he was in control of himself and scarcely needed the placating hand of Lestrade upon his shoulder to enable him to explain clearly, if breathlessly, 'Please come with me, it's Professor Cathcart. I believe she is dead. Will someone send for a doctor?' Lestrade replied, calmly, 'Right ho, son, lead the way, for it so happens that Dr Watson is here, so take us to the scene of whatever has happened.' Lestrade had often in the past demonstrated his lack of that perception that would make him a talented detective. But his placidity when under fire which was even now being demonstrated rather explained how he had risen to such a high position with the force.

We were led into what appeared to be a large laboratory with all of the scientific and medical equipment that one might expect of such an apartment. But the unexpected was there, too, in the presence of an anthropoid ape in a large cage, staring through its bars at the body of a woman which lay upon the floor very close by. She, too, was attired in the white garb of a doctor or scientist. I dropped on one knee beside the body, feeling the pulse first to be sure that life was in fact extinct, and this proved to be so. But I wanted to be sure, so I applied all the other usual tests including putting my ear to her heart and holding a mirror to her mouth. Just to be sure I struck a vesta and held it where her breath would have affected its flame. She was not only quite dead but as far as I could see had been so for perhaps an hour. The young man who had drawn us into this sad affair told us that his name was Septimus Young and that he was a laboratory assistant to Professor Cathcart. He explained, 'I had gone upon an errand for the professor to buy food for Monty.' He indicated the ape in its cage. 'I returned, pausing only to put on my white coat, entered the room and found her lying there. It looks as if Monty strangled her through the bars.'

Lestrade grunted and then said, 'Looks like it. Tell me, what is the heathen beast doing here, anyway?' Young replied, 'The professor was conducting a series of experiments with him.'

At this intimation Lestrade nodded wisely and said, 'Ah well, that explains everything! She took up a scalpel, or some such things to perform some horrible experiment upon him, he grabbed her through the bars and strangled her. He would have realised what she was about to be a doing of, for such brute beasts have some sort of sixth sense to make up for their lack of intellect. What do you think, Mr Holmes, does that cover everything?'

Holmes had stood well away from the tragic scene until asked directly for an opinion. Lestrade obviously wishing him to become involved he dropped to his knees beside the body and made a quick examination. Then he arose to enquire of Young, 'Is the creature normally dangerous?' Young said, 'Why no. Professor Cathcart could normally do anything with him, but of course there always has to be a first time.' Holmes gestured that I should join him in the examination and between us we made a more thorough exploration. There were bruises of discoloration on the throat, but very much more pronounced, on the back of the neck, there were two main equidistant bruises.

Sherlock Holmes looked thoughtful as he rose to his feet. 'Lestrade, I see no sign of a scalpel or any other surgical instrument. Moreover, the strangulation was performed by hands that were attacking from behind her. Long as his fingers may be, the ape could scarcely have applied pressure to the back of her neck with his thumbs, which the marks indicate, commensurate with the position of the body when discovered. If we had reason to believe that the body had been moved after she fell I might reconsider my opinion. Tell me, Young, what was the nature of these experiments?'

Septimus Young explained, 'Professor Cathcart was trying to prove her theory that the intellect of the anthropoid ape in general, and this one in particular, is far in advance of present scientific belief. She conducted various intelligence tests with Monty through the years, culminating with the use of a testing machine of her own design, rather like that employed by a typewriter operator.' The inspector interrupted, 'You mean to tell me that she was teaching this creature to type?' His tone was amazement tinged with disbelief. 'Not quite in the normal way. The machine has a great many more keys than would be usual and each of them is pictorial, and types not a single character but a complete word. For instance there is a key bearing the depiction of a banana. When depressed, the key would print the word BANANA onto the paper sheet fed into the machine. To explain it fully I would need to show you the contraption, but I would need permission to do so.'

Lestrade grudgingly agreed that Monty was no longer the premier suspect, but still insisted, 'You can never trust a wild beast. But assuming it wasn't the monkey, who killed the poor lady? How long were you away from the laboratory, Mr Young?' Septimus replied, 'About two hours.' Lestrade looked at me questioningly. I nodded to him, 'She would have been alive two hours ago, certainly.' Holmes asked Young, 'Can you consolidate your movements of the last couple of hours?' It seemed likely that the seed and grain merchant upon whom Young had called would be able to confirm his visit, and the doorman and guards could back up his account of his actions. So Holmes and Lestrade began to seek other suspects. By this time the body had been removed and we felt more comfortable to continue the investigation. There were four doors opening into the room. The first of these was that through which we had entered, another was directly opposite and proved to be the principal storehouse for the professor's drugs and equipment. The third led into a room which was alongside the site of the ape's cage and appeared to be locked. Behind the last door was a store for the ape's food, which we examined along with the main store room. Our remaining interest centred upon the locked door. Septimus took his keys from his pocket and opened it. We entered what appeared to be little more than a broom cupboard, though somewhat larger. Its contents were unremarkable (brooms, brushes, disinfectants) save for the presence there of a young man lying upon a bale of straw giving the appearance of being asleep! He blinked, then leapt to his feet in a bewildered manner, fishing a pair of thick-lensed spectacles from his warehouse coat pocket and placing them upon his rather snubbed nose. He blinked at us in apprehension and at last he spoke in a very furtive way, 'Septimus, I'm sorry, but I was up late last night and, well, I just settled down for a few minutes' rest and I must have dropped off. Does the professor want me for something?' He was wide awake now and anxious concerning his situation. Young introduced him to us as, 'Tommy Masters. He looks after Monty, cleans his cage and so on.' When Masters was told something of the events of the last hour or so I could see that he was deeply shocked, either that or he was an excellent actor. He said, 'Poor Professor Cathcart, poor lady. She was always good to me, even though I only swept up and that. Does Algy know?'

Holmes turned an enquiring glance to Young who explained, 'Algernon Bastow, the only other person allowed access to this room apart from Tommy and me. He will be devastated, he was more than just interested in the professor's experiments.'

Bastow, who was fetched from another part of the building, was obviously greatly affected by the news of the tragedy. He said, 'Poor Monty, he is going to miss the dear lady more than anyone. What will happen to the poor beast now; I had charge of him even before the professor set eyes on him. Perhaps I will be allowed to continue her work with Monty?'

We had rather lost all thought of Professor Mainwaring

and his invention and the reasons for our visit. When Septimus Young had pursued us with the news of the tragedy we had been on our way to a luncheon which had been organised for our benefit by Colonel Faversham.

However, the good colonel insisted that we refresh ourselves despite the hour being somewhat late for our repast to be considered as a lunch. Naturally the tragedy cast a cloud over everything but we all attempted to carry on with as little sensation as we could. Please do not, dear reader, expect me to give an accurate account of what the meal consisted of, I can only remember now that it was some kind of fish. All conversation, however we tried, continually returned to the matter of Professor Cathcart and her untimely death. The colonel said, 'Terrible tragedy, darn fine woman, brilliant too. Mind you, I did think that this idea of hers in trying to communicate with a monkey was a bit ridiculous, what?'

Holmes spoke at last, 'Who can say just what was in her brilliant mind, my dear colonel. From my observation the animal is not a monkey, nor yet an ordinary chimpanzee in the usual sense. It is a member of a rare sub-species of *pan satyrus* found only in one remote part of the Cameroons and referred to by the natives of that region as chowdra. There are more than eight hundred different species of apes and monkeys. I once compiled a monograph upon the subject.' Mainwaring nodded, 'I have heard something of the chowdra and have been told by zoologists that it is the most intellectually gifted of all living creatures, save for man himself. I would consider it an honour to be allowed to see Professor Cathcart's machine and to see the log books which she kept, if the good Septimus would allow.' Colonel Faversham coughed and intimated that it was not really up to anyone save himself as to who might see these things.

We walked back to Professor Cathcart's laboratory, which

was now of course guarded by the police. But they allowed us inside thanks to the colonel's authority. There, Septimus wheeled out what appeared, when he took its canvas cover off, to be a truly enormous typewriting machine. There were a great many more keys than would have been usual, all pictorial as we had been led to expect. The pictures included a banana, an orange, a glass of milk, a glass of orange-coloured liquid and others depicting food and drink. But there were less predictable illustrations, depictions of Young, Bastow, Masters and the professor herself, not to mention clouds, lightning, sun, a mouse being struck by a broomhead, a knife, a spoon and dozens of others, even a picture of Monty, or an ape that was exactly like him. Holmes was given permission to try the machine for himself. He struck smartly at the key controlled by the picture of the banana. When the paper was removed from the machine the word BANANA had been imprinted upon it in upper-case letters.

At this point Lestrade returned from Scotland Yard accompanied by another plain-clothes detective. At first he was inclined to poo-poo the whole possibility of the typing chimpanzee but eventually, having tried the machine for himself, admitted the possibility.

On the way back to Baker Street, Lestrade explained that during the time when we had (to quote his very words) been feeding our faces, his officers had made some more enquiries. These had revealed that Tommy Masters had been seen leaving the laboratory at a time which could make him a suspect. This did not of course make itself probable as we had ourselves discovered Tommy asleep in the smallest ante-room. How could he have got back into that apartment for us to discover him? Lestrade had to admit his witness suspect but still considered Masters as a possible murderer. 'If I had a little more evidence I would arrest him.'

Holmes was quiet over his dinner, and quieter still afterwards, seating himself upon a cushion and surrounding himself with all his available research material concerning apes and monkeys. He puffed away at his favourite clay; he was in a deep reverie from which I could not have disturbed him even had I dared. I retired to my bed until awakened at an unearthly hour by a rough shake. 'Watson, I believe I have solved the mystery of the educated ape and his murdered mistress! What time have you?' I consulted the repeater at my bedside, 'Four of the clock almost to the minute.' He almost barked, 'Too early, but at the soonest possible opportunity I must contact Lestrade, and then we must go to the war office experimental premises again.'

At six, Billy was sent to fetch Lestrade just as quickly as this could be arranged. It was eight-thirty by the time the Yard man arrived, in a rather crusty temper. 'Mr Holmes, could it not have waited another hour? My wife was furious when I was whisked away to the Yard without being able to even sample the excellent breakfast that she had prepared.'

In the hansom, Holmes questioned Lestrade carefully regarding his witness report of the coming and going of Masters. 'What did your eye-witness actually say?' Lestrade sighed, 'He said he saw him entering the laboratory carrying a load of straw for the ape's cage, just about an hour before we were summoned by Young.' 'Your witness saw his face clearly?' 'Why, no, he was carrying a load of straw, but it had to be him because he was wearing a warehouse coat, not laboratory white.' Holmes smiled, 'So all we know for certain is that a person wearing a warehouse coat with straw concealing his features entered the room at a time which makes him likely to have committed the crime. Was he seen leaving?' 'Of course not. You saw him yourself, fast asleep on the straw in that small room!' Holmes smiled with satisfaction and said, 'I did indeed.'

Colonel Faversham was happy enough to give his permission for the demonstration that Holmes outlined to him. He joined Holmes and me, Lestrade, Young, Bastow and Masters in the laboratory of the late Professor Cathcart. Only Masters seemed a little surly concerning the whole enterprise, saying, 'Hasn't the poor beast gone through enough in the last couple of days? He should be left quiet for a while.'

The colonel glared dismissively at Masters and signalled for Septimus to bring Monty out of his cage. The ape was brought forth on a collar and chain. I was struck with the very manlike way in which the animal walked and noticed that his face seemed full of simian wisdom. Monty was led up to a small stool situated before the typing machine and clambered up obediently. At first he struck the keys without enthusiasm. Tommy spoke to him. 'What does Monty want?' The ape morosely struck the key depicting himself, then a picture of outstretched monkey hands, third the picture of Professor Cathcart. The paper was removed from the machine and shown to us. There were three words, MONTY WANTS MUMMY. Tommy made a fuss of him and Algernon Bastow stroked his head and said, 'There old chap, mummy is not here. How about something to eat or drink?' But the ape shrank away from him. Bastow said, 'He's well out of sorts, poor little chap.'

To my surprise, bearing in mind his earlier enthusiasm, Holmes suggested that the ape be given a rest and that we should try him again later. Monty was put back in his cage and we left the laboratory. As we walked away from that apartment, Holmes clutched at his pockets and announced that he had left his pipe behind. He borrowed the key from Faversham and rejoined us all two or three minutes later.

We took a delayed breakfast at the insistence of Faversham and recommenced our meeting in the laboratory an hour later. This time, Holmes suggested that we all stand well back in order to make Monty less nervous or from feeling threatened. I must say I found this rather surprising, but we all agreed. I realised that there had to be a good reason for Holmes making this request. Moreover, he insisted that he should himself handle the ape and ask him a question. We found this suggestion less easy to accept (after all, Bastow or Masters would surely have had more control over the beast which would also feel more comfortable being questioned by those he knew), but could not think that any harm could come from it.

Holmes took hold of Monty's chain and directed him to the stool. The anthropoid performed this action in a rather uninterested fashion, as if he were fast losing patience, and I considered that the loss of Professor Cathcart was affecting him more than we had anticipated. He ignored Holmes's words at first, but then the detective rapped out his question again, 'Monty, who killed Mummy?' The ape screamed and hit out with a forefinger at several keys in rapid succession. Holmes took the paper from the machine, having first depressed a key which would release it from the roller. He held the paper high, in triumph, as if afraid that Monty might find some way to retract his message. He walked across and handed it to Lestrade. 'Please read aloud that which Monty has typed upon the paper, Inspector'. Lestrade looked keenly at the large typed characters and read aloud, 'ALGY KILLED MUMMY.' There was all save a quaver in his voice as he enquired, 'Which keys did he hit to produce this, Holmes?' He was told, 'The one depicting Mr Bastow, that showing a mouse being crushed by a broom and the picture of Professor Cathcart.'

There was a silence and moments of complete inactivity which seemed to take minutes to pass rather than the few seconds involved. Then Bastow sprang into action, grasping a stool and making to bring it down over the ape's head. Monty dodged the blow and the laboratory assistant screamed, rather than shouted, 'You wicked ungrateful creature, you have ruined everything. If you had the sense I have always thought you to have, you would have seen through this and kept your knowledge to yourself. I would have got you back and we could have continued the work I started . . . yes, it was all my idea!' As he tailed off he dropped the chair and turning to Lestrade said, 'Alright, Inspector, the wretched creature has given me away . . . and why would I not kill that devious woman? When she took over this department she claimed control of my animal and my experiments. I could have been celebrated but for her. It was my idea, my inspiration and my ape!' Lestrade soon had Bastow securely handcuffed and made to walk him from the laboratory. As they left, Bastow turned and looked long and hard at Holmes and said, 'I suppose you are more to blame than Monty, Mr Nosy Parker!'

I was the first to speak after Lestrade had taken Bastow away. I asked, 'Holmes, did you suspect Bastow?' He replied, 'Yes, Watson. I had realised that the person in the warehouse coat, carrying the straw, was probably not Mr Masters. Bastow appeared to me to have some sort of motive among all those involved. Not realising that Tommy was asleep behind the locked cupboard door he attempted an impersonation. He probably did not anticipate my experiment with the typing chimpanzee, but realised that any objection to it would draw suspicion to himself. He banked on Monty lacking response to anyone save himself or Professor Cathcart.' Faversham interrupted our converse, 'I found it surprising that the beast responded to you, Holmes, to the extent of typing that message of accusation.' We all nodded, save Holmes of course.

'Gentlemen, the ape, Monty, did not respond to my coaxing at all. He simply crashed his fingers onto the keys to provide a message quite unconnected with my question ... and here it is ...' He took a paper from the machine and handed it to me. I read aloud, 'MONTY WANTS BANANA.'

Faversham tugged at his neat grey moustache and said, 'I don't follow, I thought that you had already handed the message to Inspector Lestrade?' Holmes smiled and said, 'I handed him a message which he read aloud, but it was not the one that Monty typed. Earlier, when you had left me here to retrieve my pipe I typed the accusation myself, and taking the paper from the machine I placed another sheet of paper over it and fed them both back onto the roller as if they were a single sheet of paper. When I released the roller pressure I removed only the sheet I had typed myself.'

Faversham was a little worried, 'But good lord, man, your deception would hardly stand up in a court of law!' Holmes chuckled, 'It will have no need to stand, for by this time Lestrade will have a signed confession from Bastow!'

Of course the whole episode, the tragic death of Professor Cathcart and the educated ape was not anything which would under normal circumstances have involved Sherlock Holmes, who remarked to me ironically, 'Another unlikely story for your *Strand* magazine collection, Watson. It might recompense you a little for being unable to breathe a word concerning Professor Mainwaring and his wonderful engine. But then I know that such an intention had not even vaguely crossed your mind.'

In taking our farewells of the professor we were ill-prepared for his parting words, 'Mr Holmes, Dr Watson, you cannot live with a cherished marriage partner for many years and suddenly lose all interest in her, no matter what the circumstances of the parting. You have solved for me a horrific enigma which threatened my destruction, yet in the doing you needed to reveal that Mary, whom I loved and respected, was one of my main would-be destroyers. I am troubled in my mind lest she was forced into a position where she had to obey my enemies without any desire to do so. The Mary I knew would no more have tried to hurt me than fly to the moon.'

Holmes looked ruefully at Mainwaring, 'My dear Professor, I have to tell you that I think you are now beginning to look back in time through rose-coloured spectacles. Espionage is almost always indulged in for personal gain, of either money or power. Those who have patriotic fervour, or have been blackmailed, are rare in such enterprises. However, if it will help to put your mind at rest, I will make some investigations regarding Mrs Mainwaring and her part in the affair. Please do nothing of the kind yourself and follow all advice from Colonel Faversham concerning your own safety.'

Over a late meal at Baker Street, Holmes commented upon the possibilities concerning Mary Mainwaring. He said, 'My first feeling is that she was an adventuress, even before she married the professor, and did so with sole intention of assisting in its theft.' I asked, 'Do you think she could have known of its importance or even believed in its eventual perfection at that stage?' 'No, Watson, but she might already have been the pawn of others who knew Mainwaring's capabilities and wished to learn more about his activities.'

A further meeting with Mainwaring was arranged a day or so later in the form of a dinner at Simpson's. The professor was accompanied by an escort of two plain-clothes men from Scotland Yard. As we sat and toyed with our quail he said, dolefully, 'They go everywhere with me, which is why I seldom go beyond the confines of the experimental centre. You have spotted them I expect, seated at the third table on your left?' Holmes nodded, 'Oh yes, and at another table near the entrance you will perhaps have noticed two other men who have been following Watson and myself a lot lately.' I had not realised that we were under observation and asked, 'Are they Lestrade's men, too?' Holmes smiled grimly, saying, 'No, I wish perhaps for once that they were. No. I believe they are agents of Royston and Saunders and their like; but it has suddenly occurred to me that we might make use of them. Do you, Professor Mainwaring, still carry a picture of your wife upon your person?' He said, 'Why yes, I have a photographic portrait of her inside the lid of my watch. Why?' Holmes spoke very quietly, 'Do not look directly at the men I have mentioned. They are foolish enough, I feel, not to realise that I am aware of their presence. Now, how good an actor are you, Mainwaring?' He said, 'I'll try to follow your instructions.' The detective said, 'Very well, then. In a moment I want you to take out your watch and show me the portrait of your wife in such a way that they can see what it is that you are showing me. Then I want you to take out your handkerchief as if you were about to weep, dabbing at your eyes and so on.' The professor nodded and, taking out his watch, he opened it to show Holmes the picture, making sure that the portrait would be in clear view from those whom we wished to be our audience. Sir Henry Irving would have been proud of the performance which followed. Mainwaring, I swear, produced real glistening tears which ran down his face. He took the kerchief from his top pocket and dabbed at his eyes. Then he returned the cambric to its pocket and sat, hanging his head sorrowfully.

After perhaps a quarter of an hour the two men got up and left. I asked, 'Do you think they took your bait, Holmes?' (For I had some idea of what was in his mind.) He said, 'Oh yes, they will report back to their employers and within an hour there will be plans afoot to reunite Mainwaring and his wife. All we have to do is watch the agony columns. By the way, Professor, that was a wonderful performance, especially when you stared into the brightest gas-light until you produced those tears.'

It was a day or so later when I entered the sitting-room at Baker Street to find Holmes surrounded by newspapers. He tossed one of the loose sheets to me, where he had ringed an advertisement in the personal column with a red crayon. It read, 'Engine Man forgive your Canny Pest. Seven, Thursday night.'

I enquired, 'You think that Mary Mainwaring has inserted this clearly coded message?'

Holmes said, 'Well, those who control her have clearly inserted it and it barely qualifies to being in code. But then the German secret service were never very good with cyphers. The name Engine Man clearly refers to Mainwaring, suggested by his invention, hardly in code at all.' 'How about the message?' He smiled, 'Seven, Thursday gives up all attempt at a hidden message.' 'How about Canny Pest? What can that mean?'

Sherlock Holmes showed me a note pad upon which he had been writing, or scribbling to be more exact. There were a number of rearrangements of the letters of the two words, culminating in the two short words NANCY STEP. I shrugged, 'What could that mean, something to do with a clog dance?' He chuckled, 'I think not. If you recall your Dickens, Watson, there is a flight of stairs beside the south bank of the Thames at London Bridge where in *Oliver Twist* Nancy betrayed Sykes and Fagin. It has since been known by most locals and visitors as Nancy's Steps. Drop a couple of letters and you produce the name of that spot. Royston, Saunders, or even the Kaiser himself, would have known that I would pick up on that. Well, they will not be disappointed. Mainwaring will be there and without Lestrade or any of his other protectors, save ourselves.' I protested, 'Surely they will not walk into a trap, and with so few to protect him Mainwaring would be in real danger of being captured.'

'I think not, Watson, for he will not be there in person, or at least not where he will be seen. He will be concealed below London Bridge, behind the supports and with your good self as his protector. You have so often remarked that I should have been a professional actor. I believe that in Mainwaring's clothes I could impersonate him so that even his wife would not know the difference at the distance of a few yards.' I could not draw him out further at that particular time and he spent the next hour or more playing wild airs of, I am sure, an entirely original nature. But just when I felt that I could stand no more, he relented, playing Greensleeves with remarkable sensitivity.

Thursday dawned bright and it was arranged that Holmes would travel very openly from the government experimental station, disguised as Mainwaring. He would make his way to London Bridge where he would take up his position at the top of Nancy's Steps. Mainwaring, in Holmes's deerstalker and Inverness cape, would be hiding alongside myself beneath the bridge. We would all be stoutly shod and I would be carrying my service revolver. We were to have no official police escort, for it was felt that Lestrade and his ilk would become rather obvious and ruin the whole enterprise.

We managed to evade our well-meaning protectors, the professor and I, and could see no sign of them as we stood waist deep in water watching the tall figure in the wig and high-wound scarf. Holmes's prominent nose had been altered somewhat with putty and from where we stood at least the effect was quite startling. Mainwaring could not see the likeness, but then we never picture ourselves as others truly see us.

Suddenly, Mainwaring grasped my arm and whispered, 'There she is, there's Mary!' And indeed the figure of Mrs Mary Mainwaring appeared upon the bridge and started towards the disguised Sherlock Holmes. He made no demonstration, just stood outlined against the skyline at the top of the steps. As she neared him there suddenly appeared the figures of Royston and Saunders. Believing Holmes to be Mainwaring they seemed obvious in their intent to capture him. With Mary Mainwaring midway between themselves and Holmes, Royston whipped a revolver from his pocket and raised it, levelling it at Holmes and saying, 'This way, Professor, if you please.' She shouted at Holmes, 'You had better do as they say or they will surely kill you!' Holmes, far from advancing upon them, began to retreat. Royston brought his left hand up to steady the right which held the revolver and I heard the click of its safety catch. Throwing all caution to the winds and fearful for my friend's life I took out my service revolver and shot Royston clean through the right shoulder. He staggered but did not fall, and Mrs Mainwaring turned from her situation near to Holmes and rushed back to Saunders, shouting, 'My own heart, tell me that you are not dead!' She threw herself before him as if to protect him from my further shots. Then the three of them took to their heels and Mainwaring pulled at my arm to prevent my shooting them in the legs as I intended. I was for giving chase, but Mainwaring restrained me and the disguised Sherlock Holmes did not move from his position at the top of the steps. It was indeed quite a while before any of us moved. When we did, it was to climb into a hansom. On the journey north and westward nothing was said concerning Mrs Mainwaring, though Holmes did say that she and her co-conspirators would be pursued by those who had shadowed us.

Later, the three of us discussed the events of the evening back at Baker Street over a reassuring refreshment. As Holmes nudged the gasogene bottle in Mainwaring's direction he asked, 'You are, I trust, convinced now concerning your wife and her future status in your life, Professor?' Mainwaring nodded ruefully, saying, 'I could not believe that she was so concerned for the safety of that traitor and not at all worried if I lived or died. All is over between us, assuming that I am able to keep well out of her way. I will devote all my time and energy to my work. I am grateful to you for resolving my dilemma. It has all made me sad but at least I know where I stand.'

We did not see anything of Professor Mainwaring for several months, and then it was quite by chance that we met him again. It was at the Regent's Park Zoological Gardens where Holmes and I had been strolling in that strange mixture of park and prison. We had admired the sleek tigers without comment and the lion cubs, which would have usually brought the most undemonstrative of men to the utterance of expression of joyful awe, left Sherlock Holmes quite calm and unaffected. He expressed admiration for the intellect of the African elephant which purloined various articles from the pockets of his keeper. 'You see, Watson, she has no use for the artifacts that she steals, but she knows that the performance will produce buns and nuts from an admiring audience. Yet what does on in her mind? A great deal judging from the size of her skull. Ah, if she could only speak; perhaps there would be a queue of persons bringing her their problems.'

It was in the monkey house that we came upon Professor Mainwaring, leaning upon the rail which kept the public from venturing too near to the large chimpanzee cage. After the usual exchange of niceties and mannered greetings he gestured towards the animals within the cage. I noted that there was a mob of a half-dozen young chimps who scampered and played together. But in the corner of the cage sat a solitary animal of a slight variation in appearance, suggesting a sub-species. Holmes recognised the creature at once, 'Why, it is our old friend Monty!' We called to him by name but he did not respond, being dull of eye and listless in movement; a classic case of an intelligent animal with too little to occupy his mind. The urchin chimps would occasionally direct their insulting behaviour towards him, throwing missiles or screaming and slapping at him with the pink palms of their hairy-backed hands.

Professor Mainwaring, who was also a prisoner as the presence of two dark-coated protectors disclosed, said, 'Mr Holmes, Dr Watson, you see before you the dreadful result of too much education!'

In the pleasant zoo restaurant, as Holmes and I partook of iced confections usually consumed by more juvenile patrons, I asked, 'Do you think Mainwaring was referring to his own situation rather than poor Monty's?' Holmes pushed the confection away from him and started to fill his pipe, saying, 'Both, my dear Watson, he referred to both.'

It was some six years later when I was staying with Holmes at his retreat in Sussex before the subject of Professor Mainwaring and his wonderful engine was again discussed between us. The picturesque village of Fowlhaven betwixt a backdrop of the Sussex downs and the crumbling cliff-edge as a front cloth had always seemed an unlikely last abode for one of Holmes's temperament. Had I been asked a few years earlier to hazard any guesses concerning Holmes's retirement my first thoughts would have concerned the unlikeliness of such an occurrence. I confess that when he had confronted me with the news of his withdrawal from the practice of crime consultancy I had been utterly amazed. When he had further explained that he intended to keep bees in Sussex my wonder only grew.

We sat in the cool of the evening outside a hostelry, sampling the local brew from pewter tankards. I said, 'Well, Holmes, I really must congratulate you upon the new skill you have acquired in the local sport of shove-halfpenny.' He started, 'I don't recall telling you anything about my prowess in that rural Sussex delight, Watson. Have you been practising my methods?' I smiled enigmatically and said, 'I have observed the layer of hard skin on the pad of the palm below your right thumb. This could only have been produced by frequent sharp contact with the edge of a table.' He smiled with delight, asking, 'Of course you did not notice the engraving near the top edge of my tankard . . . "To Sherlock Holmes, in recognition of his mastery of Shove-Halfpenny. Presented by his fellow Fowlhaven Shovers." Really, Watson, your eyesight has lost little from the years, and you have become more devious in my absence!'

He chuckled at my attempted deception, then became more serious. 'Do you remember the little matter of Professor Mainwaring and his engine, and how we managed to help him to regain his identity?' 'Of course, how could I forget? When the weather is about to change I still suffer twinges in my left leg from that leap from the hotel window at Ville-Aesop!'

Holmes nodded, and then dramatically unfurled a copy of the Brighton *Argus*. There was a headline on the very top of the front page: BRITAIN NO LONGER AN ISLAND! He said, 'You see, Watson, some aviator in a Bleriot monoplane has actually flown the Channel for the first time.' I retorted, 'But it's not the first time. The Professor flew the Channel with his engine fitted to a Voisin, at least six years ago!' He said, 'You know that and so do I, and half a dozen others know. It was not Mainwaring's engine involved in this famous official first. By this time I'll wager our friend has produced other engines that will do more than just fly the Channel. Our lips are still sealed, Watson.'

Yes, and sealed they remained and have remained this many a year, for Mainwaring's even more greatly improved engine all but put the seal upon the winning for our country of that terrible conflict of 1914–1918 which has come to be called the Great War. Sherlock Holmes served his country, too, as I have already documented in the adventure which I somewhat dramatically entitled *His Last Bow*. As a medical man you can well understand that I was fully occupied with the victims of air raids and other wartime casualties. As it transpired, those events of August 1914 far from represented my friend's last bow as my readers will testify. When the war was over, Sherlock Holmes was offered everything from medals of valour to actual titles. As ever, he refused such distinctions, but we did go to Buckingham Palace, Holmes and I, to see Professor Mainwaring created a knight of the realm by King George. Later, we held a small celebration dinner for him at Simpson's in the Strand. He was self-effacing as ever and presented Holmes and myself with magnificent gold watches.

He said, 'My dear Doctor, the thought of watches came to me when I remembered the battering that old hunter of yours used to take. I can never repay either of you for what you did for me. But I can replace that which is now enjoyed by a Breton onion man!'

Holmes coughed and changed the subject. 'What are you working on currently, Professor, that is if no secrecy surrounds it?'

'Well, I'm involved with a rather interesting project. You will know of course that within a very few years now every home will have its very own receiving apparatus so that matters of importance, such as news and even entertainment, can be enjoyed by all.'

I said, 'I have heard something about this wireless, as I think they call it, but surely this is as near to being perfected as is possible?'

'Correct, Doctor. But can you imagine the invention being combined with a visual apparatus which could add pictures, rather like those shown by the cinematograph, being combined with the sound received?'

'Beyond the bounds of possibility, surely?'

'Not as impossible as you might think, Doctor. I have been collaborating with a Scottish engineer named Logie Baird who seems to think that it can be done.'

Holmes joined in the conversation. 'Good lord, Mainwaring, does this mean that everyone will be watching a box in the corner of the room at those times when they would normally be relaxing with a copy of *The Strand*? Well, well, at least it will mercifully spare us any more *Adventures of Sherlock Holmes*!

Mainwaring winked at me and said, 'I wouldn't bank on it, Mr Holmes!'